Kat and The Halloween Costume Caper

Kristin Riddick

In This Together Media
New York

Published in the United States by In This Together Media, New York, 2013

www.inthistogethermedia.com

BISAC:

1. Girls & Women- Juvenile Fiction. 2. Halloween (Holidays & Celebrations) – Juvenile Fiction. 3. Friendship (Social Issues) – Juvenile Fiction. 4. Imagination & Play – Juvenile Fiction. 5. Action and Adventure – Juvenile Fiction. 5. Fantasy & Magic – Juvenile Fiction.

ISBN- 978-0-9898166-1-8

eBook ISBN- 978-0-9898166-0-1

Illustrated by Nick Guarracino

For David,

The only person with whom I want to use my magic beans.

CHAPTER 1:
The Queen of Halloween

And the winner of the Totsville Elementary Halloween Costume Contest . . . for an epic sixth year in a row, is . . . Kat McGee and her Bride of Frankenweenie costume! Come on up and claim the Golden Mask. Kat McGee? Kat McGee, are you out there? Kat McGee? KAT MCGEEEEEEEE!

Kat McGee woke from her vivid and marvelous daydream to find her science teacher, Mr. Huckabee, shaking her shoulder.

"Kat McGee! Do not sleep in study hall! If you're not going to study, you should get on home. I'm going to call your mother about this. Always falling asleep in study hall!" Mr. Huckabee shook his head in disappointment.

"Sorry Mr. Huckabee," Kat said, grabbing her things and running out the door. Thank goodness he woke her up! She didn't have much time to get to the Totsville Town Hall. Today was big. Today was huge. Today was the day that could change her life . . . forever.

For Kat McGee, the countdown began every year on November 1st: three hundred and sixty-four days until Halloween. There were a few highlights along the way: Christmas, of course, as her North Pole adventure had solidified her love for that holiday; St. Patrick's Day, Chinese New Year, Easter, Diwali, Fourth of July . . . Okay, more than a few highlights. She was, quite simply, a sucker for holidays. But Halloween blew the fireworks off the Fourth of July. It even knocked the stuffing out of Thanksgiving. Kat McGee was hopelessly devoted to All Hallow's Eve.

Halloween was tops for Kat because she was tops at Halloween. See, being Kat McGee was not always easy. She finally outgrew her nickname, Kat McPee, from an unfortunate roller-coaster incident way back in the first grade, but things were still tough. Her long, curly, mousy brown hair sometimes looked like a bird's nest when she tried to control it. She was clumsy, like when she tripped in science class and spilled everything from her biosphere all over Cesar Galan, the most popular boy in her grade. She wasn't as smart as her sister Hannah or athletic like her brother Abe. In fact, she had six brothers and sisters who were practically perfect, and they loved to tease her when she wasn't.

Which was most of the time.

But Halloween was different. Kat was a grand champion trick-or-treater and could get to more houses than any of her brothers and sisters. She could out-bob any apple-bobber at the school carnival. And don't even get her started on costumes! She never chose the most popular costumes like Katniss from *The Hunger Games* or Bella from *Twilight*. Instead she invented her own.

Kat could transform anything into a treasured costume. Tin foil, cardboard, a piece of rope, and an old sheet became a sword, tie, and robe for her Jujitsu Princess in the third grade.

Last year, she worked her way into a red and white striped Candy Cane Witch: She washed and dyed an old pair of her brother Abe's discarded Little League socks three times, construction paper from her sister Emily's trashed art project became stripes on the broom, and her sister Polly's old karate uniform and pipe cleaners were repurposed into a cape and hat.

Each year, Kat used anything she could grab or find to make herself look and feel strong or beautiful, smart or interesting, funny or brave . . . all of the things she wished she could be the rest of the year.

And it worked. Starting with her Casper the Fluorescently Friendly Ghost in first grade, Kat had won the Halloween Costume Contest at Totsville Elementary for an unprecedented five straight years. Kids knew who she was at Halloween. She had *friends*. The year she was a green crayon two of the most popular girls in her class, Caitlin Williams and Zelda Goldfinger, wanted to be other crayon colors!

One of her proudest moments came in third grade when some younger kids copied the Brainy Bumblebee she'd made the previous year. After she won the Golden Mask last year, Davis Herring even came up to her and said, "Impressive McGee. You're like the Queen of Halloween."

Halloween was the one time of year she felt awesome. And she did it all on her own. She didn't need help from any of the people who made fun of her the rest of the year.

This hallowed holiday would be no different. For her first year at Totsville Middle School, Kat had created her best costume yet: the Bride of Frankenweenie. After saving Christmas, she felt unstoppable. How could she not win?

Her brothers and sisters were so sick of hearing her talk about it. *Yeah, yeah, yeah, we get it, Kat. You're going to win again. So what? Enjoy it while it lasts.* Even though she pretended to be annoyed, Kat heard something in her sister Hannah's voice when she spoke. Hannah sounded almost jealous, and Kat couldn't help but like the flip of pride in her stomach. She *was* the girl who ruled Halloween.

But now something—actually *someone*—was threatening to ruin it all. And not just for her, but for everyone. The town of Totsville, Maine, was under attack. The menacing and mean Dr. S hated Halloween.

With the bushiest black eyebrows and a huge mustache to match, Dr. S was a cross between the Swedish Chef's evil twin and the Hunchback of Notre Dame. Some kids swore they'd seen bugs of all shapes and sizes crawl out of that mustache. A poof of black and ashen hair peeked out from under his tattered black top hat. His huge, bulbous pink nose made him seem as though he always had a cold, and his protruding belly and slightly hunched back made him look even more like the big-time fun-crusher that he was. His voice, deep and frightening, sounded even scarier with his unidentifiable accent. But the icing on the scary cake was one long, fang-like tooth that seemed to be about two inches from you whenever he spoke. Most kids had only heard the words "Git outta my way!" or "Leave me alone!" come out of his mouth. Everyone was more than happy to oblige.

Other than his utter distaste for Halloween, no one knew much about Dr. S. Now, he was a hermit who hid away in his dilapidated house at the top of Hidden Meadow Hill, but rumors circled that he used to be a scientist and had invented something that made him a lot of money many years ago, before Kat was even born. He moved to Totsville as a young man, bought the beautiful old Kirkwood Mansion on the outskirts of town, disappeared into it, and let it slowly decay. Now it was just a shadow of what it had been, creepy and scary and haunting.

When Dr. S did appear once a year, he was a man on a mission, and his mission was always the same: to end Halloween. He ventured into town a few weeks before October 31st and lobbied the town council at their monthly meeting to end Halloween. At first, people just laughed. Why would they ever end Halloween? That was crazy talk.

But then things started happening in Totsville, and Dr. S's evil plan gained momentum. Two years ago, the beloved Totsville Ten-Forty, a restored old train caboose from the first train ever to pass through town, was almost destroyed by vandals on Halloween. The police never found the culprits, and Dr. S started telling the adults how dangerous it was to let their kids out after dark. He accused them of being bad parents who "allowed their kids to terrorize neighborhoods" and "exposed them to unnecessary danger" and "scared innocent children."

That year, a couple of the council members actually supported Dr. S's ban, but they were outvoted.

Then, last year, a bunch of kids became so sick from eating so much candy on Halloween that they had to miss school for two days. That really got Dr. S going. He said it was all because of Halloween, the holiday that made their children sick, literally.

Coupled with the vandalism incident, people started seeing Dr. S's point. For Kat, this was the most shocking and potentially devastating twist of all. But sure enough, last year the council's vote at the October meeting was almost tied.

Dr. S clearly hated Halloween, and he was slowly influencing the most prominent adults in the community to hate it too. Even though Totsville usually prided itself on how festive it was for holidays—the Fourth of July Picnic, the St. Patrick's Day Parade, and especially the Fall Harvest Festival were events the entire town enjoyed—a veil of apathy covered the small town in the wake of Dr. S's campaign.

Events this year had added more fuel to his Halloween-banning fire. A few weeks ago, strange things started to happen: Smashed jack-o-lanterns appeared on the streets every morning, decorations were torn down in the middle of the night, and costumes even disappeared off store shelves.

Times had changed. First, the members of the council had laughed at Dr. S. Then they were a little scared of him. And now, it seemed to Kat, they were joining him in making everyone scared of everything.

So, just one week before Halloween, many of the die-hard, tried-and-true Halloween fans and all the Halloween-haters anxiously awaited the results as the Town Council met to vote on the ordinance one more time. Kat couldn't miss it.

"We must save Halloween. We must save Halloween," Kat muttered, pacing frantically around the living room, waiting for the news conference on television to announce the council's decision. She'd wanted to be downtown to hear the results live, but her mother insisted she come straight home after Mr. Huckabee called about the study hall incident. To her surprise and complete bafflement, no one in the McGee house seemed to be bothered by the events taking over the town.

"What's the big whoop?" Polly asked from the couch, without looking up from her phone.

Gus joined in, "Yeah, we can just download the Halloween app. This game's more fun than Halloween ever was, anyway." He went back to playing his own game of *X Combat 47* on his tablet.

"Are you guys crazy? The end of Halloween! No more ghost stories, no more trick-or-treating or hay mazes . . . no more COSTUMES!? This is catastrophic!" Kat looked at them like they were aliens, but they were so mesmerized by their video games that they didn't notice. Kat shook her head in disbelief and turned around as the news reporter came on the screen.

"We have just been informed that the Town Council of Totsville has approved the ordinance to end Halloween. I repeat: There will be no more Halloween effective immediately. Dr. S, who spearheaded the movement, is on his way out now."

The reporter tried to catch up with the surprisingly quick waddle of Dr. S and pushed her microphone toward him. "Dr. S, how exactly will the end of Halloween be enforced? Don't you think you're disappointing a lot of children?"

His fat hand swatted the mic away. With his head still down, he muttered, "Git out of my way. Leave me alone."

The news reporter looked confused. She turned back to the camera and stuttered, "Well, umm, apparently Dr. S has some unfinished business. We will have reactions from the citizens of Totsville after this break."

Kat slammed the remote down and screamed, "NOOOOOOOO!!" She ran into the kitchen, almost knocking over Gram. In her distraction, she'd forgotten all about her date with Gram to bake Gram's famous black cat cookies for Halloween. On any other day, Kat would be front and center, helping.

Kat's grandmother, Gram to all who knew and loved her, was the only person in the family who totally understood Kat. Only Gram thought Kat had potential all year long. Only Gram could make her smile on a rainy day. Only Gram didn't make fun of what everyone else thought was her mostly-average, normal-to-mediocre, nothing-spectacular, middle-child way of doing things. Gram made Kat feel special, regardless of what day it was. And even though she lived far away in Seattle, she always seemed to show up for a visit when Kat needed her most. Kat couldn't have been more thankful that she was here now.

"They . . . they actually did it. They t-t-took it away," Kat sniffled as she held back tears. "There isn't going to be a Halloween. No costume contest. Nothing. I'm back to being a no-body."

Gram enveloped Kat in a big bear hug. Even the wonderfully familiar scent of peppermint and evergreen from Gram's sweater couldn't change the sense of doom and utter sadness Kat felt.

Gram lifted Kat's chin and wiped away a tear, "Cheer up, buttercup. You know, it isn't always about winning. You're always special to me, with or without a costume."

Kat pulled away. "You don't understand. I was good at this. Halloween was MY holiday. This was *important*."

Gram looked at Kat and shook her head, smiling sadly at her. "Kat, one of these days you'll understand how important *you* are. But you know when things look the worst, that's when something special could just POP up!"

With that, Gram pulled a lollipop with a tiny orange pumpkin atop it from behind her back.

"Thanks, Gram, but I don't feel like eating—"

Gram cut her off and took a step back. "Now, now Kool Kat. You're not going to turn down my homemade pumpkin pop? I made it just for you, and I'm almost positive it will make you feel better." She winked and held it out.

Kat didn't think anything could make her feel better. But if anyone could do the trick, it was Gram. Only semi-reluctantly, she accepted the pop and studied it. It was a perfect miniature of a pumpkin, complete with a little twig-looking stem on top and creases from stem to bottom.

She licked it and tasted honey and pumpkin and cinnamon . . . and something else that she couldn't quite put her finger on.

"Hmm. So many different flavors," she said, looking at Gram and taking another lick, "but still delicious."

"Well, they say it takes a lot of small pieces to make one amazing puzzle," Gram said in her usual sweet but cryptic way, as if she were giving Kat a secret and Kat had to figure out what it meant. She handed Kat a few black cat cookies and gave her another hug. "Let me get back to baking. Go enjoy your pop and cookies," she said, a smile on her face and a twinkle in her eye.

"Thanks, Gram," Kat said, licking her lollipop. She headed upstairs to her room in the corner of the fourth floor. Was it the taste of toffee or a sliver of syrup? Kat couldn't figure out what made the lollipop so tasty and so unique, but she couldn't get enough of it.

She closed her door, thinking about what Gram said. Most of her old costumes were laid out on her bed; Kat had pulled them out earlier thinking they would inspire her into action. She sighed as she looked down. They weren't much help now, with Halloween banned. The pink and green polka-dotted Preppy Pirate from kindergarten looked small; Jujitsu Princess was a little dingy; even her Candy Cane Witch costume looked dated. But still, Kat couldn't help it: She cherished them all, and she was sad that after turning her closet and the attic inside out, she still couldn't find the Green Crayon costume or her Casper the Fluorescently Friendly Ghost.

Next to her old costumes, was her latest and greatest triumph, the Bride of Frankenweenie. She had worked on it for weeks, and Gram had helped her finish just two days ago. Kat had made it up by combining two of her favorite Halloween movies, *The Bride of Frankenstein* and *Frankenweenie*. She made a papier-mâché hot dog and painted it with borrowed paint from her brother Ben's forgotten art set. She found an old big black wig and cut, ironed, and straightened it until it stood straight back. Instead of a white stripe, like the Bride of Frankenstein, she made a yellow Silly String stripe that was puffy and looked like mustard. No one could beat her. This costume would help Kat make her mark in middle school.

But now it lay neatly beside the others, ready for a day that might not happen. A wave of sorrow hit Kat. She had to think of a way to stop this horrible ban.

Kat grabbed her backpack and shoved the cookies Gram gave her and a couple of her costumes inside. Maybe if she went downtown, she could show the council her costumes, plead her case, and be back by dinner. She finished her pumpkin pop, put her backpack on—and suddenly felt a little dizzy and a lot sleepy. Kat half-walked, half-swayed towards her beloved cats Salt and Pepper. Maybe she should wait until morning. Her entire body felt like a Slinky.

Slumping down on the pink and purple beanbag Gram had given her for her birthday, her eyelids drooped. They felt so heavy! As her eyes started to close, Kat almost forgot about what Dr. S had done to her hallowed holiday.

CHAPTER 2:
Treatsville

Kat opened her eyes to find herself in a sea of orange. She felt itchy, and quickly realized she was not on her beanbag at all but a bed of hay. She heard sounds too: a sneeze, a chortle, humming, a cough, a snicker. Kat sat up drowsily and looked around. She couldn't figure out who or what was making the sounds, but she was in the biggest pumpkin patch she had ever seen.

Every shape and size of pumpkin imaginable surrounded her: fat and round, skinny and tall, as small as a marble, as big as a blimp. She heard another laugh and looked to her right: no one.

The pumpkin in front of her started to wiggle. The one to her left started to whistle. *Oh my,* Kat thought, *it's the pumpkins. The last time I woke up in a strange place I was at the North Pole with Santa and Sadie Claus, so maybe this is happening? Maybe I'm not dreaming?*

She closed her eyes, counted to three and opened them again. Nope; still surrounded by pumpkins making a cacophony of curious sounds.

"You're right. You're not dreaming."

The deep, sultry voice came from above her. Kat snapped her head up and saw a woman in a tight, long black dress with a

13

big black beehive atop her head. She smiled down from the top of one of the largest pumpkins, which seemed to be expanding and deflating like a giant breathing balloon. The woman had dark, kind eyes, ruby red lipstick, and a matching feather boa around her neck.

Kristin Riddick

How did she know what I was thinking? And is she a witch? Because I've never seen a witch look like that! Kat thought, staring at her, unblinking.

"Yes and no. Witches, except for Glinda the Good of course, get such a bad rap. I like to think of myself as a Maker of Magic and Mischief," the woman said. A sly smile spread across her face, and she uncrossed her legs. The pumpkin shrank, as if commanded to deliver her to the ground, then inflated back to its original size. The woman landed right next to Kat, who saw that she was wearing the most dazzling deep purple, sparkling high-heels.

"Can you read my mind?" Kat asked in disbelief. "And how do you walk in those? Who are you? Where am I?"

"Hmm," her voice was as smooth as silk. "I knew you'd be inquisitive, which is loooooovely." Everything the woman said mesmerized Kat, as if her voice was a magical lullaby. "To answer the first, in a way, yes. To the second, I don't really walk unless I have to. I float. And finally . . . call me Dolce." She held out her hand. "And you're Kat. *Enchante'.*"

Kat struggled to get up to reach for Dolce's hand, but tripped over a pumpkin vine, which hissed in protest. She fell and quickly hustled to get back up.

"Sorry. Two left feet." Kat dropped her head, embarrassed.

Dolce lifted Kat's chin with a long, purple fingernail, "Not at all. You're just what we expected, and exactly what we need. Your Gram was right about you."

A breeze swept past, bringing a chill to the air. Dolce's tone grew more urgent. "Oh no. Not again. We must go, quickly and quietly. We need to get you out of here and to safety."

Dark clouds suddenly gathered above and around them. Dolce looked at Kat and put a finger to her lips. Kat was overwhelmed with curiosity and fear and excitement, but remembering her North Pole adventure, she stayed silent. Dolce turned and started towards the gate, floating.

I have a choice, Kat thought. She could sit here in this weird and increasingly cold pumpkin patch, which seemed to be alive, or she could follow this woman, who was magically floating in the air. *Um, no-brainer.* Kat ran to catch up.

The scarecrow at the edge of the fence held a sign that read, "Treatsville: A hop, skip and a jump," with a blinking arrow pointing to the right. Kat thought she saw the scarecrow wink at her as she passed, but she tried to concentrate solely on keeping up with Dolce, who floated out of the patch and down a tree-lined path through a forest.

It was impossible to keep up, though. Kat realized she was still wearing her backpack, which she remembered putting on right before she fell asleep. It felt lighter somehow, and yet this was harder than the mile run in the physical fitness test at school!

As she started to slow, Dolce turned and blew her a kiss. Kat thought that was cheeky for someone she'd only known for three minutes, but then she looked down and saw that her feet were no longer touching the ground. She was floating right behind Dolce. Wow! Floating through the air was like riding in Santa's sleigh without reins or reindeer or (the more she thought about it) *anything* between her and the ground.

Kat gulped and kept her eyes on Dolce's feather boa, which wiggled in the breeze behind her. Dolce seemed amused by Kat's wide-eyed mixture of fear and curiosity, and smiled warmly at her as they continued their flight down the path.

Now that she wasn't worried about keeping up or tripping over her own feet, Kat began to soak in her surroundings. The leaves of the giant trees were falling in a flurry of glowing golden yellow, burnt orange, and beautiful deep red. As they drifted down, the glow turned into a twinkle, and sparkles from the leaves jumped off before they hit the ground. A leaf softly landed on Kat's shoulder. It smelled like cinnamon and nutmeg. She put the twinkling leaf into her mouth: It tasted just as it smelled! And it melted quickly on her tongue.

An edible leaf? Kat thought. *What is this place?*

Dolce's pace quickened, and Kat saw a clearing up ahead.

They floated out from the forest into an enchanting and strange world. A huge violet field gave way to another field of pink and another of silver. The fields extended as far as the eye could see in a rainbow of colors: dark blues and bright reds, deep oranges and vibrant greens. Every field was not only colorful but filled with something fantastic. Orchards of different shapes and colors spread across the fields: apples and oranges dotted the trees, of course, but passionfruit and pluots and jelly beans and gumdrops also grew on or fell from the trees. Kat saw patches of pumpkins making all sorts of hullabaloo, just like the field where she'd woken up. Beside them, fields of jack-o-lanterns glowed warmly. Campfires were burning, with s'mores roasting themselves in midair.

Cottages of lollipop sticks and gingerbread houses dotted the lane. Huts made of hula skirts stood next to Lincoln Logs lodges, each house more unusual than the next. A sign pointed to Witch's Brew River, which circled through the village and flowed under Bubble Gum Bridge. A zigzagging Scary Stream of dark chocolate twisted through the forest, with planks made of Legos to cross it. Streets were paved with SweeTarts and lanes were made of licorice. Haunted houses stood on every corner. Cauldrons were strewn about, and brooms were lined up like bikes on a bike rack.

At first glance, Kat thought they'd stepped onto a movie set or were looking into a painting; these things didn't seem real. As intriguing as it all was, there was no movement. Silence and stillness filled the air.

Then Kat saw what looked like the Wicked Witch of the East appear out of nowhere, grab a broom, and disappear again. Before she could blink, something with a long red cape shot out from above a bed of murmuring pumpkins and flew into the forest. Whatever it was looked a lot like Superman.

As Kat looked more closely, she saw bursts of color and movement in front of her; they disappeared just as quickly into a cottage or under a bridge. She had to pinch herself—she couldn't believe what she thought she saw. Was that Tinkerbell flying with Peter Pan into that ice cream igloo? That couldn't have been Snoopy and Charlie Brown peeking out from inside the doghouse made of chocolate chip cookies. Kat had to grab Dolce's arm to steady herself, because it looked like these were *costumes* that had somehow come to life. She'd put her own costumes in her backpack, so she grabbed it and looked inside. Sure enough, none of them were there; only a few of Gram's black cat cookies remained. Kat looked up at Dolce, bewildered.

Dolce threw her head back and gave a deep, radiant laugh. "Kat, welcome to Treatsville—Where Costumes Come To Live."

Kat was speechless.

Dolce smiled. "Let's keep moving. Take my hand. I want to make sure you are close to me at all times."

As they floated through the village, Kat saw more living costumes. Strawberry Shortcake stared out through the curtains of a strawberry cottage. Inside the windows of the Hall of Justice, the superheroes Aquaman, the Wonder Twins, and Captain Caveman gathered in a circle. A goblin and a zombie ran by and disappeared into an alley. Cheerleader Barbie and Fashionista Barbie ran right in front of her with Beach Party Ken and slammed the door of Barbie's Dreamhouse. Every costume she saw was life-size. They had arms and legs and heads and faces, just like Kat had seen hundreds of times in books and on television. But as Kat looked more closely she realized that every costume was unique. Every one was different. Every one was special.

Dolce saw the look of realization on Kat's face.

"That's right. You won't find twenty-seven R2D2s here," she explained. "There is but one. Each is a reflection of how you, Kat McGee, know and see it. Costumes come and go every year, so when they aren't with you, they're here."

Kat could hardly find the words. "This . . . this is . . ."

"Magical. Halloween is the one day of the year during which the real and the magical meet, but here in Treatsville, Halloween is alive each and every day. The real and the imaginary are all around you."

Kat looked more closely at the costumes, trying to hear what they said or see what they were doing. After her initial shock at witnessing such a wonder, she realized something was off. The scene was almost gloomy. Why did they look scared? Were they hiding from her? Most of the costumes she saw wouldn't even look her way. Kat slowly recognized the looks on their faces: a mixture of sadness and fear.

Kat looked up at Dolce but didn't say a word. Dolce put her arm around her and sighed. "You're right. They *are* scared, and sad, too. What you see is a skeleton of what Treatsville used to be, and not in a good glow-in-the-dark Skeletor costume kind of way." She tried to smile. "I wanted you to see what was left of it before it was gone completely."

Dolce's head snapped up. She looked suspiciously around and pulled Kat closer to her. Everything stopped. Kat felt the same chill that had descended upon the pumpkin patch creep into her bones, and soon it engulfed everything. The few costumes that were still outside disappeared in a flash—into houses, through the forest, into the sky. The Three Little Pigs ran into their tiny brick house and bolted the door. They passed the Monster High kids as they chained the doors of their Monster Student Lounge shut.

"Hurry! We must get inside before it's dark," Dolce whispered and tightened her grip on Kat's hand.

The wind picked up. Darkness and fog enveloped them. Kat felt almost suffocated and tried hard to catch her breath. Thank goodness she was somehow still attached to Dolce's invisible magic carpet. Dolce picked up the pace as they glided down Black Licorice Lane, the main street, passing costumes hurrying into homes and stores, anywhere they could find shelter. The Head Goblin of the Ghost and Goblin Haunted House School turned his sign to CLOSED; the blinds in Wonder Woman's Wig and Mask Repair snapped shut. The Cowboy and Ballerina peeked out from behind the curtain of the Haunted Saloon, but hid as soon as Kat and Dolce passed.

Finally, they came to a giant tepee at the edge of the forest. They got there in the knick of time. The sun had vanished, the wind was howling, and the fog had completely covered the village and surrounding fields.

This tepee didn't look like an ordinary tepee in the Old West or on a campout with the Totsville Scout Tots. It was made of black and deep purple velvet, and it sparkled intermittently, like lightning bugs in a darkening sky. Kat hesitated as Dolce pulled back the curtain door to enter, but she was cold and scared and thought whatever was inside had to be better than what was out here. Feeling as if she was going to be swallowed whole, Kat took a deep breath and ducked in; Dolce looked back once more at the village and followed.

Inside, Kat saw only a small round table before the curtain fell behind them, and the room was left pitch black.

"Don't be scared, Kat," Dolce reassured her, squeezing her hand. "Darkness is our friend, and it is only as scary as you make it."

The large, dark figure gazed intently into the glowing jack-o-lantern in front of him and watched the girl and the witch disappear into the sparkling tepee. He'd seen enough.

He placed the pumpkin's top on the jack-o-lantern. The scene disappeared, and the evil-faced pumpkin slowly came back to life.

"I told you she would find another to try to defeat you," the grimacing jack-o-lantern said.

"She can try . . ." the man grumbled, twirling his thick black mustache between his thumb and forefinger. He sat in the chair in front of the talking jack-o-lantern. An evil smile crossed his lips. "But she vill not succeed."

Kat looked up. Instead of the top of a tepee, she saw a sea of stars in a clear night sky. Dolce puckered her lips and looked down, and Kat felt the ground fall out from under her. She started to fall, slowly and lightly, as if she were on a feather. When she softly landed, candles hovered around the room, and Dolce smiled beside her in the low light.

Looking around, she felt as though she was in a genie's bottle. Her toes sank into a soft and fluffy carpet—*where were her shoes?* A couch of pillows lined the circular room. Dolce sat back on a poufy black cloud-like chair suspended in midair and pulled her legs up beneath her. It was the most comfortable-looking chair Kat had ever seen, which made her think of her beanbag. Dolce blew another kiss in her direction. A second later, Kat was sitting in an overstuffed beanbag, a little fluffier and furrier than hers at home, but nonetheless inviting.

There she goes again, reading my mind, Kat thought.

"I know, I'm sorry." Dolce smiled as she confessed. "I want to make sure you are completely comfortable, because what I have to tell you is very serious."

She leaned forward, and her smile disappeared.

"We used to love darkness descending on Treatsville. That's when all the fun begins on Halloween, right?"

Kat wasn't sure how to respond, so she just nodded slowly. She could have sworn she saw bright eyes blinking in the darkness behind Dolce, but turned her head back to the mischief-maker and focused.

"But this fog, this darkness, is different," Dolce continued. "You see, Treatsville came to be thousands of years ago. Our purpose was to fight off evil and harmful spirits, much like the origins of your world's Halloween. In your world Halloween began as a celebration of a symbolic door opening between the real and the spiritual worlds. Spirits could pass between the two one last time. Treatsville grew and flourished because a door from your world opened to ours. All of the good parts of Halloween discovered this passage and found a home here."

Kat was completely enthralled.

"In your world's Halloween, people wore costumes to protect themselves from spirits who were between the land of the living and the underworld. Here the costumes protected Treatsville from the invasion of evil spirits who wanted to cause harm. In return, the costumes had a place in which they felt safe. They banded together in a place that was *all* about the good aspects of Halloween, except it was every day instead of one day a year.

"When costumes aren't needed or wanted in your world, they come here. Here, they can be at their best. Once a year, those who are called return to your world. For you, costumes are just one part of the fun of Halloween, but here, they *are* the magic. They are the heart and soul of Treatsville."

"Then why do they seem so scared? What's wrong with them?"

Dolce sighed and explained, "What you saw out there is grim indeed. Treatsville used to be the most dynamic place you could imagine, day or night."

As Dolce spoke, a cloud appeared above her head like a cartoon, and Kat saw exactly what Treatsville once was, a town even bigger and brighter, with thousands of costumes milling around, not just the few she'd seen behind bushes and curtains and doors: Buzz Lightyear and Woody, Indiana Jones, Angry Birds, Transformers, Ninja Turtles, Cinderella, Princess Merida, Goldilocks and the Three Bears, Smurfs, dragons, a butterfly and a caterpillar, Monsters, Inc., C3PO and Han Solo . . . any and every costume, floating or jumping or rolling or laughing or playing or frolicking around the wondrous world of Treatsville. To Kat, it looked like the most magical giant playground she'd ever seen.

"Costumes were at their best then," Dolce continued. "We played games all day and told ghost stories every night under a luminous full moon. We lived, breathed, did everything, for Halloween. Halloween was in all of us."

Dolce paused. The images above her head of better days in Treatsville disappeared, and a darkness and fog drifted through the cloud. Kat knew what was coming next was not good.

"But there is an evil man . . . a horrible, bitter man, who lives at the top of the hill on the edge of town. He is the reason

Treatsville is covered in a blanket of fog and fear. He used to be a very important part of our town, but he disappeared, and he's back for revenge. He turned his back on us once. Now he wants to destroy everything we hold dear, everything that is special about Halloween."

Anger swelled in Kat's chest. Someone was trying to ruin Halloween here too? "How?" she blurted. "Why? What is he doing?"

"He's stealing costumes."

Kat jumped to her feet. "What?!?"

In the cloud above Dolce's head, the fog cleared. Kat watched costumes running around, locking doors—and finding traces of their friends, left behind: a crown from the King of Hearts, a boot from the Long Ranger, Captain America's shield.

"The Headless Horseman was the first to go," Dolce said. "The entire Addams Family was taken in the span of five days. And we don't know if GI Joe was kidnapped or went rogue." She shook her head with concern.

"I don't know how he gets them to leave Treatsville, but with every one he's able to capture, the fog gets thicker. The air gets chillier. And each time a costume disappears, a little more magic seeps out of Treatsville. With no costumes, we have no defense against this menace. It usually happens at night, which is why you saw all the costumes running inside frantically, although we've heard of daytime disappearances, too. It's why you'll see groups move together. We've found safety in numbers.

"But every time you feel that chill, it means he's stolen another from our midst. He's stealthy and sneaky and eluded my efforts to catch him in the act. Without the other costumes, those remaining don't have the magic or the energy left to try to find and rescue them . . ." she trailed off, and added sadly, "This afternoon you saw the only costumes that remain. No costumes, no magic. No magic? No Treatsville."

"What do you mean?" Kat asked.

Dolce dropped her head and whispered, "If we don't get the costumes back by midnight on the eve of Halloween, if they can't make it over to your world Halloween night . . . the dullsville of Treatsville will become permanent."

"Why?" Kat asked.

She looked at Kat and said gravely, "Halloween magic will disappear. Your world will have no Halloween, and without the costumes to give us Halloween magic, Treatsville will cease to exist . . . *forever.*"

The cloud above Dolce disappeared in a poof. Kat found herself staring into darkness. She could hardly see the stars now.

"The end of Halloween in Totsville has basically already happened," Kat said numbly, sinking back into the beanbag, remembering the news conference.

"I know. Which is why I thought you might be the one. Your Gram and I have discussed what's happening in Totsville. We thought you, more than anyone, would understand."

That's twice she's mentioned Gram, Kat thought.

"Oh, we go way back, your Gram and I," Dolce said with a wink. "And she and I both believe you may be the only one who can do this."

"I don't understand. Do what?" Kat asked, confused.

Dolce turned around, and spoke into the darkness. "Come here, my little one."

The bright eyes Kat thought she'd seen earlier emerged from the darkness. They were attached to something with the body of an owl and the floppy ears of a rabbit, its color as dark as night, its lavender eyes the size of fish bowls. Dolce stroked it, and it purred like a kitten.

"Meet DeLeche. DeLeche, this is Kat." Again the owl purred.

"Show our friend Kat the Snaggletooth," Dolce almost purred back to the owl.

"Snaggletooth?" Kat didn't like the sound of that.

DeLeche's lavender eyes closed. When they opened, they resembled two crystal balls, fogged over. The mist cleared, and Kat saw a gigantic house at the top of a hill. It was dilapidated and windows boarded. Its huge iron door slowly opened.

Kat walked closer to the owl to get a better look. She couldn't believe what she saw.

The man coming out of the door donned a tattered black top hat. A pouf of black and ashen hair peeked out from beneath. Kat noticed his hunched back and protruding belly next. He pulled out a handkerchief and wiped his huge, bulbous pink nose. His bushy black eyebrows and matching mustache made Kat lose her balance as she jumped back in disbelief.

"It—it—it can't be," Kat gasped.

Dolce nodded. "I know. Snaggletooth is menacing, isn't he?"

Kat stammered, "N-n-n-ooo. I mean, yes. But . . . it's just that . . . well, he looks like someone I know."

"I'm afraid there are Halloween-haters everywhere. And Snaggletooth's power reaches far and wide," Dolce said sadly.

Kat put her head in her hands. It was happening all over again. She was going to lose Halloween twice in one day! Kat jumped up from her beanbag and practically screamed, "But he can't do this! It's not fair! People need to see the good parts of Halloween!"

Dolce smiled at her and said, "That's perrrrfect. We need that kind of spunk and enthusiasm. I knew you would be able to help save us from Snaggletooth."

Kat frantically circled the tepee. What was happening? Why was she here? Why did this monster hate Halloween so much?

And what could she possibly do to help? She didn't know any magic.

She looked at Dolce. "You have all these powers. Why can't you fight Snaggletooth? Can't you just cast a spell to get the costumes back?"

"I wish I could, Kat," Dolce said, impressed by her insight. "Believe me, I've tried. But Snaggletooth is smart. When he concocted the spell and was able to take those costumes, he knew that the essence of Halloween magic lay in the heart and imagination of a child. Only children completely understand and appreciate it, so only a child who truly believes in that magic will be able to break his spell. Only a child can take the costumes back from him and return them to Treatsville, restoring it to what it was.

"I've recruited many children from around the world, but none have had both the heart *and* the courage to complete the task. We need you to break the spell of Snaggletooth. Kat, we need you to save Halloween."

Kat started biting her nails, which she only did when she was nervous; this Snaggletooth seemed even worse than she imagined Dr. S to be, since she had never actually met him. Was he Dr. S's equally evil twin here in Treatsville? She could never win against someone as scary as Dr. S who also happened to be some sort of diabolical wizard.

But it was Halloween. She couldn't just sit by and watch it disappear forever. She had to do something. The second she had doubts, she remembered Sadie Claus, the tenet of wisdom, and the spring in her step from the candy fruit. Everyone had believed in her at the North Pole, and when Kat had confidence she was able to save Christmas. If she could save Christmas, could she somehow save Halloween too? She was the Queen of Halloween, after all.

Dolce stared at Kat with her dark, mysterious eyes. Those eyes made Kat believe Treatsville needed her. Deep down, she knew what she had to do.

"Let's talk about this spell."

CHAPTER 3:
The Spell Of Snaggletooth And The
Halloween Handbook

"It's not going to be easy," Dolce warned as she led Kat from the lavish genie bottle room into the darkness. They didn't open any doors; the space simply opened to them. Surprisingly, Kat was not afraid.

They walked into the darkness of what seemed to be a narrow hallway, and Dolce suddenly stopped. A large rectangular glass case descended from above. As it stopped, hovering before them, Kat saw a thin, black leather bound book inside. She reached out to touch the sparkling gold lock, but sparks flew from it when her fingertips got close.

"This book is protected by the Spell of Sweetness," Dolce said matter-of-factly. She blew a kiss towards the shiny translucent case and the book rose straight through the glass, as if it wasn't even there. She held it admiringly. Kat thought Dolce looked like she was protecting an ancient treasure.

"It is an ancient treasure to those of us who call Treatsville home," she said, still knowing Kat's thoughts exactly. "This," she paused dramatically before she continued, "is the *Halloween Handbook.*"

They started to walk through the darkness, and pictures and videos appeared beside them on walls Kat couldn't see, as if they were walking past a line of drive-in movie theatre screens.

"You see, for hundreds upon hundreds of years, Treatsville never had to fear threats like Snaggletooth. But many moons ago, when I was a wee witch-in-training, Treatsville faced another evil spirit in the Battle of the Blob. He was one of those lost souls caught between the world of the living and the underworld of evil, and he didn't appreciate the Halloween goodness that Treatsville embodied."

Beside them visions of costumes fighting off multiple menacing blobs of vapor and smoke appeared. Dracula and a Caveman costume battled an eerie black fog-like mass, tension, anger, and fear written across their faces.

"Everyone fought over what spells to cast or concoctions to make in order to protect the costumes and Treatsville," Dolce continued. "But my great grandmother, my Maker of Mischief and Magic mentor, Sucre, came up with some very simple lessons."

On the wall beside Kat, a witch with a high grey beehive who looked like an older version of Dolce appeared holding a book in her hands.

"The entire village learned these lessons and was victorious in the Battle of the Blob. The lessons were sealed in this book in case any threat ever arose again. Sucre passed the *Handbook* on to me."

Dolce stopped walking and turned to Kat. Her voice became graver as she said, "When I learned Snaggletooth was behind the disappearances and realized what he was trying to do, I knew we had no defense. That is when I started to recruit kids, kids just like you who love Halloween, to help defeat him.

I have shown this handbook to many children from all around the world . . . but all have failed."

As she talked the wall behind her showed kids running down a hill screaming or jumping into Dolce's arms. One small boy with a huge afro, sporting a tuxedo T-shirt and board shorts, started crying just looking at the *Halloween Handbook.*

"Some kids don't even have the courage to open the handbook. Unless you are truly ready, the lock will . . ." Dolce hesitated, but continued. "Well, it will surprise you. It won't open for just anyone, but once open, the book will help prepare you."

"For what, exactly?" Kat wanted clarification.

"What all these kids have failed to do. The only way to break the Spell of Snaggletooth . . ." Dolce paused. "Is to trick-or-treat—"

"That's it?" Kat interrupted. "All those kids ran screaming and crying from trick-or-treating?! Because I am the best of the best. I mean, a true professional. You've never seen—"

It was Dolce's turn to cut her off. "Oh, dear one, this isn't your run-of-the-mill suburban foray for treats. We have plenty of costumes capable of doing that. No, no. Our most special Halloween enthusiast, you," she turned and smiled at Kat, "will use the *Halloween Handbook* to learn how to travel through the Forest of Fear . . ."

The moving pictures on the wall changed to show a dark, petrifying forest with red-eyed creatures, fanged animals, moving tree limbs, and a trail of mud and moss that looked alive.

"Around the Pits of Gloom . . ." The wall showed giant holes in the ground, but there was nothing visible inside; Kat could only hear moans coming from deep within them.

"Over the Swamp of Sorrow . . ." A bubbling tar-like swamp taunted Kat as though it was burbling out, *I double dog dare you to come here.*

"And up the Hill of Haunts to Snaggletooth's lair."

Kat stopped and turned toward the image of the ominous house at the top of the hill. The foreboding iron door loomed high above, looking completely unreachable.

"There you must say trick-or-treat to him, showing your belief in the true magic of Halloween, and bring the costumes home to Treatsville before midnight of the start of Halloween." Dolce stopped and pointed at the image of Snaggletooth that appeared beside her. "Beware: Snaggletooth won't let them go without a fight."

More pictures of children appeared, flashing across the wall. Dolce sadly explained them one by one: "Carmen from Mexico made it halfway through the Forest of Fear, but got tripped up and ran back with a bloody nose. Nina from Nevis almost made it to the door, but someone, or something, scared her so much her teeth chattered for a month." Dolce was silent, clearly remembering each unfortunate episode. Kat watched each failure on the wall, and it was daunting. She didn't want to be one of those kids.

Dolce snapped out of her dreamlike trance and looked directly at Kat. "Don't underestimate the gravity of this mission, Kat. I love the spooky and scary, but Snaggletooth is . . . ghastly. And smart." Dolce puckered her lips and made a smacking sound. The images disappeared, and in a blink they were back in the genie room, candles lit and beanbag inviting Kat to take a load off.

Dolce perched herself on the cloudlike throne, holding the handbook. "The *Halloween Handbook* can teach the willing volunteer the lessons you need to know to conquer all of these things. But you have to use it wisely and figure out how it will work for you. The path to Snaggletooth's is different for everyone. Yours will be unique, and I won't be able to help along the way. And the clock is ticking. Only three days until Halloween."

Dolce sensed Kat's hesitation. "Or you could go home, Kat." The disappointment in her voice made Kat's heart sink. "But if you do, Snaggletooth will win. He will destroy Halloween and Treatsville."

Kat couldn't decide. She wanted to help Dolce and Treatsville, but more importantly, she *had* to have Halloween, wear her Bride of Frankenweenie costume, and win the costume contest. While she loved a good adventure, she also knew the Forest of Fear alone would eat her alive.

Still, Halloween was *her* holiday, her time to shine. Without it, she'd be a nobody all year long. She wasn't going to let a scary guy in a creepy house ruin it. If saving Treatsville meant saving Halloween, she had no choice: she had to find a way to defeat Snaggletooth.

Kat took a deep breath and, before she could change her mind, said, "I'm in."

Dolce let out a siren's sigh of relief, a soothing song that—strangely—made Kat realize she was exhausted. As usual, Dolce was two steps ahead. She blew a kiss straight up into the air, and a luxurious bed appeared with a big soft comforter and more pillows than Kat could count.

"Can't fight demons and the dark side when you're drained and weary," Dolce said, placing the *Halloween Handbook* next to the bed. The room darkened, except for a soft yellow glow that surrounded the handbook. "We'll start fresh first thing tomorrow."

Dolce looked at Kat's nervous face and spoke calmly, her words relieving and somehow tranquilizing. "You, Kat McGee, are going on a journey that will change everything . . . for you and for us."

Kat closed her eyes and nodded. Dolce was right.

She only hoped that change would be a good one.

The house atop the Hill of Haunts was every bit as scary as it appeared on the walls of Dolce's magic tepee. With the giant, rusted, iron door, the boarded windows, and the dead trees surrounding it, the house looked abandoned, gloomy, and threatening.

A hulking figure, hunched over like a wilting stem, trudged up the old, rickety spiral staircase, his hands crossed behind his back. He unlocked a heavy, dusty door and walked into a large, dark room, in which a single chair sat facing a torn black curtain. He reached up, threw back the curtain, and stared into the dark space. There was movement, a few whimpers and gasps.

"SILENCE!" his voice boomed. The movement and sounds stopped abruptly. "So . . . she zinks she's found another one."

The creepy sound of his unidentifiable accent caused more shuffling and a few groans.

"AHHHH HA! HA!" His sinister laugh rang out. "I've got to hand it to zat defiant witch. She does not give up."

He paced back and forth across the length of the room, talking into the darkness. "I vill have to find out more about zis one," he said maliciously.

He paused, turned and sat in the empty chair, facing the darkness. His voice, now low and menacing, probed, "And I bet some of you vill be able to help me."

He leaned back, crossed his fingers over his protruding belly, and flipped the light switch beside him.

Staring back at him, chained, bound, innocent, and scared silent, were almost all the costumes of Treatsville.

CHAPTER 4:
The Recruits

Kat woke up so cozy and comfortable that she half-expected Gram to be sitting next to her bed with a cup of hot chocolate ready to talk about what kind of good dream she'd had.

But instead of Gram, the first thing Kat saw when she opened her eyes was DeLeche, perched inches away on the bed, his looming lavender eyes staring straight at her. She jerked upright in surprise; DeLeche, unfazed, simply scooted to one side so her flailing arms wouldn't knock him in the beak or off the bed.

"Geez Louise, DeLeche. You scared the bejeezus out of me!" Kat exclaimed. She sat back on one of the plethora of pillows and let out a breath she didn't realize she'd been holding. Then a soft yellow gleaming drew her eyes to the small wooden table beside her bed.

The *Halloween Handbook*.

So she didn't dream it. She really was in Treatsville, in some kind of bewildering tepee-slash-genie-bottle owned by a witch—no, what had Dolce called herself? Oh right, a *Maker of Mischief and Magic*.

Kat felt a vague sense of dread in the pit of her stomach. Everyone was counting on her, Kat McGee, to save Treatsville from the evil Snaggletooth. She slowly started to freak out. *What on earth was I thinking? It's not like I'm part of the X-Men. I make costumes with super powers, but I don't actually have any.*

DeLeche's eyes closed and reopened, transforming into the two crystal balls. When the fog disappeared, Kat looked into those eyes and saw scores of costumes, alive and jumping, flipping, playing, rolling, strolling, tricking, running, twirling, and sneaking around Treatsville.

Dolce, in the way only she seemed to be able to do, snuck up behind Kat without scaring her. She put a hand on Kat's shoulder and leaned down. "That's what Treatsville could be again, Kat. Look at the Little Mermaid and Nemo in Witch's Brew River. See how much fun Katniss and Peeta can have when they're not actually in the Hunger Games? It could be like the good ol' days."

Kat put her head in her hands. *If only the costumes could go with her.*

Dolce snapped straight up. "Oh dahhhhling, what a brilliant idea! You could recruit costumes . . . of course! I knew you were special. No one else has ever thought of that," Dolce gushed as if Kat had actually spoken the words.

Kat perked up and looked at Dolce, practically yelling, "Really?! This changes everything!" She threw the covers off, popped out of bed, and grabbed her shoes.

"I'll take Wasp. She's not in the movie, but she's one of the most important of *The Avengers,* in my humble opinion." Kat paused and reconsidered. "Honestly, any of the Avengers will do."

Dolce's expression changed, and her smile faded.

"I'm sorry, Kat. It's a fabulous idea, but your choices are limited, and honestly, you won't find many able to help you." She sounded genuinely sorry to have rained on Kat's parade.

Kat stopped and sunk down onto the bed. "What do you mean? All those costumes out there . . . Why can't some of them come with me?"

"Most of the costumes are gone or missing, and those that remain just don't have the strength or the magic anymore. Snaggletooth has seen to that."

Kat was confused. "But I thought you said—"

"You can definitely recruit a couple of costumes," Dolce explained, trying to find the right words, "but I'm afraid the costumes that are most affected by what's missing from Treatsville are those that are the most popular with children around the world. They have the most magic to lose, so they're weaker than the others. You'll have to find costumes that aren't as trendy or beloved. They may have some magic left, and if you can convince them to join you . . . " Dolce didn't sound convinced, but for Kat's sake she continued. "Maybe they can help you along the way. They won't be in top form, however, so more than two may be difficult to manage. The *Halloween Handbook* will help you, but they're going to need a little . . . encouragement."

Kat panicked. "Difficult to manage? Encouragement? *I'm* the one who needs encouragement! I don't need . . . I don't need . . . *rejects!*"

Silence. They awkwardly stood in the low light of the room, as if a bomb had been dropped and neither one could talk or move. Kat was shocked and ashamed that she had said such a horrible thing. She would do anything to take away the disappointed look that Dolce was giving her.

"I didn't mean that."

Dolce's frown softened. "I know you didn't. And I know you're scared."

"I'm not scared!" Kat shouted, in a voice that said otherwise.

"Well, maybe you should be. You're going to need help. And each and every costume has something to share, Kat. I thought you knew that better than anyone. Do you think some costumes aren't worthy of you anymore?"

Kat looked at her shoes, embarrassed. "No, no of course not. I know all costumes are special. I believe that. I really do."

Dolce again lifted Kat's chin with her long purple fingernail. "You've been in training your entire life for Halloween. Remember: You can sometimes find the most potential in what other people consider rejects. You've shown that every year with the costumes you create. Now we need that creativity and intuition more than ever."

Kat attempted to smile. She thought about the North Pole and the booth of potential, and she remembered how much confidence she'd had when she returned to Totsville, and how strong, popular, and powerful she had felt when she'd won the costume contest again and again.

What was she scared of? She was so good at trick-or-treating she probably didn't need costumes at all! Who really cared which ones she took with her? She'd treat the mission like every other Halloween: She ruled the roost. The costumes would be like her assistants along the way, and this would be her grandest adventure yet. Kat smiled as she thought of this. She felt better already.

Kat's feet lifted and started to rise as if they were in an elevator. Dolce looked at Kat's face, gazed up into the darkness, and thought aloud. "That's better. I'm glad to see some of that Kat confidence back. But if you're going head-to-head with Snaggletooth, we must find you a trick-or-treat team to help get you there."

The long black curtain was pulled back, and Snaggletooth surveyed his loot.

"It von't be long now," he told them. "Soon I vill have all of ze costumes, and Treatsville vill be no more. Ah HA HA HA."

The evil laugh again made the costumes cower back. They all looked to the corner of the room, where, in a small separate cell, a weak and flattened costume lay on the floor. He had been there so long that he had almost no magic left. He could barely lift his head.

Snaggletooth looked at the cage where he kept his first and greatest victim, a reminder of how far he'd come and how close he was to achieving his goal. Just as Treatsville lost magic without the costumes, the longer Snaggletooth kept the costumes, the weaker they became. The pile of fabric on the floor of the cage, a mere shadow of his former bright and shining costume, was proof. Smiling evilly, Snaggletooth remembered his first conquest proudly.

Kat McGee and The Halloween Costume Caper

After years of work, of mixing and matching and testing different potions and ingredients like Ravenstooth Weed, Panic Powder, and Brain Fog Juice, he had finally found the perfect blend for his new candy: MAGIX. It stunned any costume that ate it long enough for Snaggletooth to grab it. Once out of Treatsville, the magic began to seep out of the kidnapped costumes like water down a slow-moving drain, leaving them weak and foggy and lethargic.

Costumes like Darth Vader and Magneto had not fought as hard when they realized what was happening. He used them and others like the Riddler and the Joker as guards, watchmen, and general assistants on his mission, giving them Halloween Hater Juice to keep them alert and strong, replacing the good magic in them with his own.

He needed to perfect it, though. He had underestimated the others' love for this wretched holiday. The magic stayed with them longer, and his potion wasn't strong enough. But it was only a matter of time. He looked at those weakened costumes now, huddled together like a bunch of scaredy cats, chained and cuffed to the wall behind the curtain.

Once Treatsville's magic was gone, he'd start them on the Halloween Hater Juice as well, and they would all belong to him . . . just like their former home.

Dolce and Kat emerged from the glistening tepee into the ghost town of Treatsville—where all the ghosts had unfortunately vanished or gone into hiding. Everything was so still and quiet. All Kat could hear was the sound of her own footsteps on Black Licorice Lane.

"What was your favorite costume, Kat?" Dolce asked, floating slightly ahead of her, the *Halloween Handbook* balanced on top of her beehive.

"Hard to say. I've loved each of them for different reasons."

"Fair enough, dear one. When have you felt the strongest on Halloween then?" Dolce pressed.

"Oh, that's easy. My Jujitsu Princess. I felt strong AND pretty, and that was the first time people really started to notice me," Kat said.

Dolce stopped abruptly and turned toward her. "People who love you don't notice you because of a costume, Katherine McGee," she said sternly. Kat knew Dolce was serious because she'd used Kat's whole name, like her mom did when Kat was in trouble. Luckily, her tone quickly changed and was sweet, almost playful, again. "But that's perfect. Princess Jujitsu. Let's see . . . where is she most likely to be?"

"We're going to find *my* old costumes?" Kat asked in surprise.

"Why not? You made them and know them better than anyone. Who better to help you tackle Snaggletooth?"

"Where are they? How will we find them?"

Dolce knowingly smiled. DeLeche appeared from behind them and flew down the lane, stopped on Candy Corn Bridge until they caught up, then continued on to the other side of the village. They passed all of the Smurfs' houses, and then a huge ship that was smack dab between the Smurfs and the house where the Wizards of Waverly Place lived.

"What in the world is a ship doing in the middle of the block?" Kat inquired.

"The costumes from the *Pirates of the Caribbean* don't like to be landlocked, They said it makes them feel better to at least stay on their ship when they're not at sea." Dolce shrugged her shoulders. "Whatever floats their boat." She smirked at her own silly joke.

They passed what looked like a railroad station, but as soon as they were upon it, it suddenly changed, becoming the entrance to a dark alley. Before Kat had a chance to ask, Dolce said, "That's the *Harry Potter* costumes thinking they're being very clever. They believe if they keep changing the façade and casting spells, it will disguise their whereabouts from Snaggletooth."

Kat thought that was a pretty good idea.

DeLeche stopped and perched upon a lamppost with a jack-o-lantern on top. It was next to a four-story house that looked strikingly familiar. As they got closer, Kat realized why: It looked just like her house in Totsville!

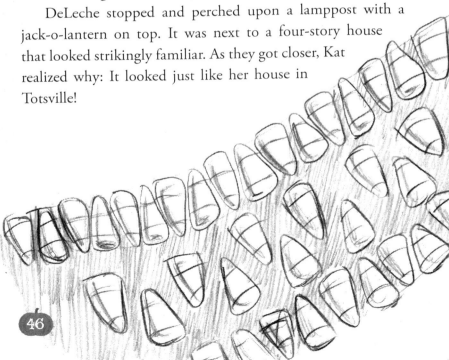

"Holy Moly!" Kat ran up the steps but soon realized this house was extremely different from her real home. The steps were made of jellybeans and the shutters of graham crackers. She turned the donut doorknob, and carefully peeked around the front door to see the familiar old green couch in the living room. But when she walked towards it, she realized the couch was glowing in the dark. And when she sat on it, it jiggled like Jell-O.

"Cool!" Kat exclaimed.

Instead of stairs there were tiny trampolines to jump from floor to floor, so Kat jumped her way up to her room in the corner on the fourth floor. She opened the door slowly and couldn't believe her eyes! It was the biggest room she had ever seen. There were not one but three or four pink and purple beanbags, beads circled and floated around the room in bright, sparkling colors; and glow-in-the-dark stars, moons, and planets seemed to be moving around the ceiling. A disco ball twirled in the middle of the room, and when Kat stepped in, it felt like the floor was made of clouds: soft, fluffy, even a little bouncy. She looked down and saw that she was covered in glow-in-the-dark necklaces and bracelets.

"This is the greatest room ever! What happened?"

"You did this, Kat. In Treatsville, we take imagination seriously. If you can dream it or wish it, here the imaginary can become real," Dolce said.

Kat looked at her humongous bed; it was identical to the one she'd slept soundly in last night in the tepee. Almost all her old costumes were there, fast asleep. All the ones she'd stuffed into her backpack that were gone when she landed in Treatsville, plus some she had completely forgotten about: Brainy Bumblebee from second grade, the Neon Moon from when she was just four years old. Just like at home, she didn't see the Green Crayon and Fluorescently Friendly Casper. Here, Preppy Pirate and Bride of Frankenweenie were also missing.

She turned to Dolce, "Where's Preppy Pirate? And my newest one, Bride of Frankenweenie?"

Kat could tell Dolce didn't want to say anything.

"We don't know for sure, but as I said, costumes disappear every day."

Instead of being sad, the news made Kat more determined. She would love to play in this new and extraordinary room, but it was time for action.

"Then we need to hurry! We need to go now! Wake up!" She yelled. "We've got to get going! We're going on a . . . " Kat hesitated, trying to think of a way to make their mission sound enticing. "We're going on a—a trick-or-treat adventure! And y'all are the best costumes for the job."

Jujitsu Princess reluctantly propped herself up on her elbow, lazily put her head in her hand, and stared at Kat. "Oh. It's you."

Kat had expected a warmer reception, but reminded herself that her old costumes had lost some of their Halloween magic and weren't themselves.

Jujitsu Princess looked at Kat, dazed and suspicious. "Why should we go anywhere with you? Do you even remember us? I'm tired, anyway," she said and closed her eyes, looking bored with the entire conversation.

"Remember you? Are you nuts? How would I have gotten over the Woodson's locked gate and around their pool without your sword?" The Princess opened her eyes again and stared at Kat. "And remember when we outran all of the third-graders and Jack Rosenberg, in his karate outfit, challenged us to a duel?"

Princess Jujitsu sat up, faced Kat, and touched her sword beside her on the bed. "We totally would have won that duel if he hadn't chickened out."

Dolce watched the other costumes sit up on the bed and start to listen. It was working! Kat had her own brand of Halloween magic, and it was rubbing off on her costumes.

"That was one of my best Halloweens ever," Kat said. "Gram said I never looked better or stronger."

The Candy Cane Witch came closer and asked, "What about me? You didn't feel good and strong with me?"

"Honestly, you were totally different. It took me a while to get everyone to realize what I was doing with you. A candy cane broom? White and red striped hat, with knee socks and a cape to match? But once they did, man, oh, man! My brothers and sisters couldn't believe I could come up with something so different and clever. It was one of my proudest creations, and got me my fifth trophy!"

The Candy Cane Witch's red painted cheeks deepened as she blushed. Kat could see her and the other costumes getting a twinkle back in their eyes.

"See? You get excited about Halloween the way that I get excited about it. You don't want to sit here and be bored and sleep and have kids forget about you, right? We need to go out there and remember what we love most. Nobody, especially Snaggletooth, can take that away. It's up to us to save the magic of Halloween!"

"But what do you want us to do? We've been in here so long I'm not sure we remember the fun of Halloween. Or even how to trick-or-treat," Jujitsu Princess said, walking over to Kat. "Besides, Snaggletooth has made it so scary that no one wants to open their doors anyway." The costumes shuddered at the mention of Snaggletooth's name.

"Yeah, and as much as I still need them, my broom and hat are kaput. They used to help me get out of any sticky situation, but now there's no magic left in them at all," Candy Cane added, pointing to her drooping hat.

Kat needed to explain where they were going and what they had to do, but she wasn't ready, and she didn't think the costumes were ready for it either. "Listen, this is going to be a very special trick-or-treat night, one like no other. We're going to have to prepare for it. I could really use the help, but I can't take all of you. Any volunteers?"

Jujitsu Princess was the first to jump forward. "I'm tired of sleeping all day. I want this to be over. Let me at him," she said, jabbing her sword in front of her.

The other costumes looked away, like Kat did when she didn't want to answer a question in Dr. Boeker's math class and was trying to avoid him calling on her.

Kat thought carefully. She was glad Jujitsu Princess had stepped up. If she was going to make it to Snaggletooth's, the Princess's strength would come in handy. And since she could only take two, Candy Cane Witch was her other best bet. Kat felt so creative and interesting and clever the year she made her. She knew Candy Cane would bring those qualities with them on their adventure.

Kat walked closer to the red and white witch, and sat down next to her on the bed, which felt like a mixture of a Jacuzzi and a cloud, soft and fluffy but almost bubbling, like it was giving her a massage. Kat pretended to talk to the group, but really focused on Candy Cane.

"This mission will definitely be scary, and it will be hard, but it will bring Treatsville back to the way it once was," Kat leaned in and whispered in Candy Cane's ear. "And once we get there, it will be the best trick-or-treat you've ever had."

Candy Cane Witch looked at Kat, reticent but wanting to join. She swallowed hard, trying to get rid of her fear. "Without my broom and hat tricks, I've felt useless. I want the magic back, too. If you're going, then I'm going."

"Awesome!" Kat felt even stronger. She was actually beginning to think this could work. The Queen of Halloween was ready to roll. She drew her costumes into a small huddle, putting her arms around the Witch and the Princess. "We don't have much time, so we're going to have to be quick, crafty, and strong. There's no backing out, no turning back. We're in it to win it."

She stood up and put her arm out in the middle of the circle. The costumes looked at each other, and then looked at Kat.

Jujitsu Princess was the first to put her hand on top of Kat's. "Let's do this."

"For Treatsville," Candy Cane Witch said, slapping her hand on Princess Jujitsu's.

Kat put her other hand on the pile. Princess Jujitsu and Candy Cane Witch followed. Kat smiled, hoping she could make this work. Princess Jujitsu leaned in to the pile of hands and said, "TEAM KAT!" Kat liked the sound of that.

With a gentle smile, Dolce floated over and put her hands on theirs.

Throwing their arms in the air, they yelled as one, "TEAM KAT!"

CHAPTER 5:
Courage Camp

Kat had stayed up half the night in Treatsville's wacky and magical version of her own Totsville bedroom. She was too nervous and excited to sleep. Dolce had left DeLeche with her to keep watch and make sure she was safe. She promised to be just a kiss away if Kat needed anything at all. Kat assured her she'd be fine. She had a lot of work to do . . .

Because when she disappeared in a poof of purple smoke, Dolce left behind the *Halloween Handbook* in all its glowing glory. Around 2 a.m., her old costumes sound asleep beside her on the bed, Kat took out the sacred handbook. She wanted to know how it could help her and the costumes prepare for all of the horrifically horrible things Snaggletooth may throw at them—but she remembered she couldn't even open it unless she was truly ready.

Kat decided to try. Before her fingers even touched the lock, **ZAP**! The lock sent a small shock straight to her fingertips.

"Piddlesqueaks!"

Kat tried to reassure herself that she was ready. She knew this was the key to opening the book. She again thought of her North Pole adventures. She remembered how she communicated with Prancer and Cupid and the other reindeer, and how happy Santa and Sadie Claus were when she returned them to safety. She closed her eyes and thought of her happiest moments: baking with Gram, saving Christmas, and . . . Halloween: beating Madison Brantley in the Zombie sack race in second grade, winning the Golden Mask for the best costume at the Halloween Carnival all five years, her siblings patting her on the back after she trick-or-treated through the entire neighborhood in twelve minutes flat . . .

She opened her eyes and touched the lock again. The glow around the handbook suddenly turned from gold to silver to purple to pink. The lock unlocked and the book flew open, flipping itself through every page, forward and backward and forward again. It landed on one of the first pages.

In thick, elaborate, and mystical writing, it said:

THE HALLOWEEN HANDBOOK: EVERYTHING YOU NEED TO KNOW TO KEEP TREATSVILLE SAFE, IN 3 SIMPLE LESSONS.

SIGN BELOW IF:
YOU ARE A LOVER OF HALLOWEEN,
OF TREATS AND TRICKS,
OF MAGIC AND MISCHIEF,
OF CREATIVITY AND ILLUSION,
OF THE COSTUMES AND CREATURES
THAT BRING US TOGETHER.
YOUR SIGNATURE IS YOUR VOW TO DO
EVERYTHING IN YOUR POWER TO KEEP
TREATSVILLE SAFE FROM HARM, TO HAVE
HALLOWEEN LIVE FOREVER.

Kat was amazed at how many names were listed below. Dolce wasn't kidding when she said kids had come from all around the world. Rohan from Rio, Pepita from Peru, Macy from Maryland, Leloise from Louisville, Mary Emma from Madagascar . . . The list went on for pages.

Before she could even think about it, a pen popped up in the air, and she quickly signed, *Kat from Totsville*. Once she did, she was able to turn the pages on her own.

As Kat read through the lessons, she knew merely reading them wasn't going to do the trick. If she and the costumes were going to defeat Snaggletooth, they needed to do some serious training. She turned to DeLeche, still at his post beside her on the bed, and asked him to send Dolce a message. Once she was satisfied with her plan, she finally fell asleep, just before dawn.

A few hours later, Kat was up and ready to go without any alarm or DeLeche hovering above her head. She looked outside and saw no sun rising high in the sky; the fog still hung like a blanket over the village. If she and the costumes didn't make it up to Snaggletooth's soon, it might never lift again. She shivered at the thought.

Kat picked up the *Halloween Handbook*, kissed it for luck, and carefully tried to fit it into her backpack. Magically, it shrank to just the right size to fit. She turned back to the costumes on her Jacuzzi-cloud bed and wondered how to wake them up. A small kazoo on the desk in the corner caught her eye. She picked it up and hummed into it, but instead of a crazy kazoo buzz, a cheery, albeit loud, voice started singing, "Good morning! Good morning! Trick-or-Treating Training begins today!"

Wow, Kat thought, *it sings my thoughts! I love this room!*

The costumes were having a harder time getting up this morning, and Kat knew she was going to have to work extra hard to keep the Halloween magic alive. Kat kept blowing in the kazoo, and the costumes kept hearing *Good morning! Good morning! Trick-or-Treating Training begins today!*

Reluctantly, they dragged themselves up just to stop the song and started shooting questions at her groggily.

"Where are we going?"

"What are we going to do to get ready?"

"When do we get to trick-or-treat?"

"What *exactly* do we need to do to get Treatsville back?"

Kat grabbed Jujitsu Princess and Candy Cane Witch. She promised the others they would be back soon, and told them to keep watch and try to be strong. As they left her fantastic magical bedroom, Kat knew she had to come clean and tell the two costumes exactly what they had to do to save Treatsville.

The three of them headed to her meeting point with Dolce on the other side of the village, and Kat knew this was the perfect opportunity.

"So, I have good news and bad news," she started. Wanting to get it out as fast as she could, she blurted out quickly, "theonlywaytosaveTreatsvilleistotrickortreatatSnaggletooth'shouse-savethecostumesandbringthembacktoTreatsville."

Surprisingly, they understood every word.

"Whoa, whoa, whoa. Wait a minute." Candy Cane Witch held out her hand to signal STOP, like a safety patrol crossing guard. "You didn't say anything about trick-or-treating at Snaggletooth's! No one's ever made it up there. Costumes have *disappeared* trying to get around the Swamp of Sorrow, never to be heard from again."

Princess Jujitsu agreed. "Yeah, and that Hill of Haunts isn't for wimps and weaklings. I mean, I could probably handle it, but it's steep and scary and I've heard that Snaggletooth has set all sorts of booby traps. How do we even know what he's done with all the costumes? How are we ever going to get them back?"

Kat saw the wide-eyed fear in their faces, but she'd been expecting this. She tried to reason with them. "You didn't let me tell you the good news."

They looked down at their feet, shuffling them like they were already defeated.

"Look, don't worry. I'm in charge here, and I'm good at Halloween. No, not good. I'm great. Sure, Snaggletooth is scary and all that, but that's why I've come up with a plan." Kat stood tall, and said excitedly, "The good news is . . . we're going to Courage Camp. All of us. And by the end, we're going to be primed and fit for anything that comes along, jumps out, frightens us, freak us out, tries to throw us for a loop, whatever. We'll be ready."

Princess Jujitsu and Candy Cane Witch looked at each other quizzically.

"Courage Camp?" they asked in unison.

Dolce was waiting for them in a field of grass that continually changed colors from black to blue to purple to navy to lavender to maroon, alternating dark shades, like a pulsing kaleidoscope of color. Hence its name: Kaleidoscope Field. As they walked toward her, she blew a kiss in their direction. A circle of mushrooms the size of armchairs, all a very dark brown, appeared around her.

"Have a seat. They're brownie mushrooms, but no snacking or you won't have a place to sit." Dolce leaned down and whispered in Kat's ear, "By the way, this is a brilliant idea. Only you, Kat, could come up with something so clever to make sure you understand the lessons in the handbook."

Kat smiled proudly up at her. Although she didn't want anyone to know, she was also very nervous. Was this was actually going to work? Last time she had a "brilliant" plan, she ended up in her brother Gus's closet, hiding from her sister Hannah because Kat's "amazing organic" shampoo had turned her hair a bright lime green.

No. I've got this, Kat told herself.

The costumes each sat on a mushroom, and Kat stood beside Dolce in front of them.

"Welcome to Courage Camp," Kat said. "We're going to embark on a series of games and tasks that will prepare us for our trick-or-treating adventure." She pulled the *Halloween Handbook* out of her backpack. The enormity of the book as it enlarged to its original size and its encircling glow made everyone gasp.

"This is the *Halloween Handbook*. I know it looks intimidating, but there are actually just three simple lessons we need to learn. Easier said than done, of course. So I've come up with a kind of camp. We'll complete exercises and activities to learn these lessons Dolce and her grandmother Sucre laid out for us. Clues to the scary or unexpected things we may encounter along the way are in this book, so each activity will help us prepare for something different."

Candy Cane Witch's arm shot up. "I'm no good without my hat and broom. Without their magic, how will I be able to help? How do we know what will jump out at us?"

"We don't know what will jump out. And I don't have a magic hat and broom either, but Courage Camp is going to train us to conquer our fears."

The costumes shifted on their mushroom seats, looking uncomfortable.

Jujitsu Princess spoke up, "What if it doesn't work?" Kat didn't have an answer.

Dolce floated forward and put her hand on Kat's shoulder reassuringly. "You won't know until you try," she said. Her soothing voice had a way of putting them at ease. "And you have Kat. She's the best of the best. Right, Kat?"

Kat nodded, suddenly feeling a lot of pressure in her chest. *Yes,* she reassured herself, *I will do what I do best and dominate Halloween!*

Dolce looked around at the graveyard of gloom Treatsville had become. "You may come running back screaming and scared," she said softly. "Or you may run back screaming and celebrating to find the Treatsville you love restored. Regardless, it's going to be a hauntingly fun ride."

The costumes didn't look fully convinced, but they were definitely curious. Jujitsu Princess grabbed a bite of her mushroom brownie chair, popped it in her mouth, and jumped up. She tried to read the first page of the *Halloween Handbook*, still hovering before them, from a distance; she didn't want to get too close. Squinting, she read, "So where do we find this Spooky Story Hour?"

Of course . . . ze Halloween Handbook. Snaggletooth thought as he peered into the jack-o-lantern at Kat and the costumes, scowling as he saw them stare in wonder at the giant glowing book. He again placed the top back on the jack-o-lantern, which grumbled.

"She's got the handbook again," Jabbering Jack grunted.

"I'm not vorried about ze book. It's ze costumes. It vas smart to recruit them to help. Maybe I shouldn't underestimate zis child," Snaggletooth snarled.

"Remember: only a child from their world can ruin your plans and stop you," Jabbering Jack reminded him.

"You don't have to tell me that, you dim-witted gourd," Snaggletooth snapped. "I'll just have to stop her and her little friends from getting out of Treatsville. Kill a few birds with one stone."

An evil smile spread across his face. He twirled his mustache and thought of a plan. This was the perfect opportunity to stop the girl *and* add to his costume collection. He couldn't have these costumes working against him.

No, he'd make them regret the day they decided to help Kat McGee.

CHAPTER 6:
Lesson One: Spooky Story Hour: Prepare For The Unexpected

TO GET THROUGH THE FOREST OF FEAR, YOU MAY NOT KNOW WHAT'S AROUND THE BEND, SO PREPARE FOR THE UNEXPECTED WITH A SPOOKY STORY EVERY HOUR ON END.

"I think this is what the first lesson is trying to tell us," Kat said as the costumes followed her into the Friendly Forest on the outskirts of the village. "We need to think of the scariest things imaginable," she said, fighting her way through the dense fog, darker and gloomier than before, even at midday. "Then we use those things to come up with the most vivid ghost stories we can. We take turns telling them, and try to scare each other silly."

The costumes stayed very close to Kat, constantly looking around to make sure they weren't being followed or trapped.

Candy Cane Witch joked, "Should someone tell a story about Snaggletooth stealing costumes from Treatsville?" Kat and Jujitsu managed a smile and soft chuckle, but her joke only reinforced the gravity of their situation and made them more cautious.

They came to a clearing where Dolce had blown a kiss and whipped up a small campfire. Kat gave Dolce a secret signal—a thumbs up and a pop! of her lips—and then joined the costumes around the fire. Dolce winked back at Kat knowingly and disappeared to ready herself.

"I'll start," Kat volunteered. "This is the story of Horrible Hannah. " She started to tell the story of Hannah, a woman who lived alone on the top of a mountainside with no one to keep her company. She terrorized the village below for years, making everyone afraid of her. People and cattle and animals disappeared and the villagers suspected Hannah was taking them up to the mountainside for sacrifice.

"BOOM!" Kat said, describing a sound a young boy heard in the night, and as soon as she said it, a huge **BOOM** came from nowhere, almost shaking the ground beneath them. Everybody fell back in surprise and shock. The costumes looked around to see where the sound had come from, but no one could be seen or heard.

The costumes moved a little closer together.

"What was that?" Candy Cane Witch asked.

Jujitsu Princess shrugged, not wanting to speak in case something really was out there.

As Kat continued the story, a soundtrack started emanating from the forest. The costumes and Kat experienced every **BUMP, SCRATCH, SCRAPE, YELL,** or **HOWL** at the exact moment Kat described it. Kat knew Dolce was making the story come to life, unseen but heard, and yet she was still startled and frightened too.

"And the story goes that when the villagers finally made it up the mountain, all they found was the skeleton of a body with long, curling fingernails, straggly grey hair, and piles of bones next to it . . . with teeth marks in them.

"And that was the end of Horrible Hannah."

SCRATTTTTCCCCHHHH. The costumes, and even Kat, cringed at the sound of fingernails going down a chalkboard.

"STOP! Make it stop, please! Make it stop!" Candy Cane Witch screamed as she crouched into a ball, practically rolling over in a mixture of laughter and the heebie jeebies. They all laughed as the sound finally stopped, and silence again filled the air.

"I'm next," Jujitsu Princess said, bringing her voice down. "I'm going to tell you the story of Lobo, the lone wolf that petrified the towns and territories all over the north country. And beware, because this really happened."

Everyone resumed their positions closer to the fire—and closer to each other. Before Jujitsu Princess said another word, they were completely surrounded by the sound of howling and crying wolves, startling them stiff.

AAAWWWOOOOOOOOOOO. . .

Jujitsu Princess started to shrink down, but a smirk crossed her face as she realized the sounds were helping her story come alive too, like Kat's, making it all the more fun. She started to feel brave, and continued. "A hunter in a small village was determined to find this wolf Lobo and kill him. He was famous for trapping and catching wolves, but this wolf had eluded all hunters . . ."

As she spoke they heard growling and then the rustling of leaves in the forest. Her story unfolded, and again the spooky sound effects made it even more chilling and ominous. Kat and the costumes hid their faces in their hands or screamed or huddled up against each other with every **SHRIEK**, **CRACK**, or **POP** in the tale.

"The wolf had frightened the hunters into a corner, and none of their weapons could save them. Lobo seemed invincible. Then, as he was about to lunge toward them, he disappeared into thin air."

A **POOF!** of smoke came up from the fire as the Jujitsu Princess recounted her story. Her audience was attentive and engaged, wondering what would come next.

Kat got the sense they were not alone. She looked into the shadows and sure enough, some costumes had crept closer from the darkness of the forest. Robin Hood and Little John heard the sounds coming from the clearing. Thinking it might be Snaggletooth trying to take one of their costume friends, they hurried to investigate. When they saw Kat and the costumes were only telling stories, they remained out of sight, but stayed to listen to the spooky tales.

A few minutes later, Kat noticed Little Red Riding Hood— and even the Big Bad Wolf!— had also joined them near the clearing. They had been hiding in the forest as well. Although hesitant to come fully into the circle, Kat could see that they were trying to enjoy the stories as they had before Snaggletooth's costume-stealing rampage began. The costumes had taken refuge in the forest, but this small circle of Halloween Magic had brought them out.

Kat saw a spark of the magic of Treatsville in these costumes, and it made her realize anew what was at stake. This was Treatsville: Where Costumes Come to Live. She and her friends had to bring those costumes back and return the magic to Treatsville, or there would be no more ghost stories. No more getting scared and laughing afterwards. No more Halloween. The thought of it gave her goose bumps.

Princess Jujitsu was finishing her story.

"And to this day, you can hear the sound of Lobo on the first full moon of the winter season, letting everyone know he is still among the living . . . a lone wolf. "

AAAAAWWWOOOOOOOO!

Kat and the costumes joined in as the howling of a lone wolf echoed out of the darkness, calling, "AAAAWWWWOOOOOOOOO!"

"We are our own pack of wolves, on a mission to destroy Snaggletooth!" Kat exclaimed. The costumes hooted and hollered in agreement.

Kat and the costumes continued to tell tales big and small. They squealed in delight as the stories got more gruesome and fiendish. And they began to realize that they were telling scary stories—but they were only stories. At the end of each one, they all were still around the fire together, unharmed and safe and having a great time. There wasn't a reason to be afraid. The costumes started looking over their shoulders, anticipating Dolce's sound effects, and giggled at their own jitters.

As the night wore on, they spouted off scary things they might encounter in the other forest, the Forest of Fear:

"Red-eyed flying foulawunks!"

"Worms that crawl up your legs!"

"Tree limbs that come to life and pull you up by your hair!"

"Monsters that drag you away by your pinky fingers!"

"Quicksand that swallows you whole!"

"Zombie costumes that have gone to the dark side!"

The list got more and more outlandish, but Kat and the costumes were realizing that their imaginations made it all worse than it was. In voicing their fears, they began to conquer them.

Kat smiled. "There are so many things that scare me, but when I say them, they aren't as creepy." The costumes nodded in agreement.

Dolce appeared from the shadows and joined the circle. They looked up at her, and she recognized something in their eyes that made her ruby red lips part in a smile.

"This is what I've been missing in you costumes. You've found your courage. When you prepare for the unexpected, you become more courageous. And Kat, you too seem to have found courage. Admitting things that scare you in order to face them isn't always easy. You're going to need that on your journey.

"Know that whatever you face, whatever may jump out unexpectedly, you have the courage to get past anything. You may need to use that soon. A few things could go bump in the night."

Dolce blew a kiss and three sleeping bags appeared around the fire. Kat and the costumes looked at each other.

"Are we sleeping here? In the forest? Alone?" Candy Cane Witch asked, her voice trembling slightly.

Dolce smiled at them. "You won't be alone. You'll have each other. What better way to test your courage? Don't worry. I'm just a whistle away." She handed Kat a whistle in the shape of ruby red lips. "If you get into trouble, blow this whistle and I'll be here in a flash."

Kat blew the whistle, but the only thing that came out was a kissing sound. Dolce smiled at her signature calling card. She blew another kiss and drinks and snacks appeared: jamberry juice, chocolate-covered Chumbawoodles, and Courage Camp bars, a special treat Dolce made especially for the occasion.

Another kiss, and a black cast iron kettle appeared above the campfire, promising delicious hot chocolate whenever they wanted it.

"That should do you until morning," Dolce said with a smile.

Kat smiled and shrugged. "No problem. We'll take turns keeping watch while the others sleep. It's just like camping out in Gram's backyard in Seattle. I'll take the first watch."

Kat knew it wasn't exactly like Gram's backyard, but she had more courage when she was with her costumes. She put Dolce's whistle in her backpack and walked around the campfire, organizing snacks and preparing herself for the first watch. Candy Cane Witch and Jujitsu Princess settled in, and Dolce blew a kiss and disappeared.

It was a good thing they were together, Kat thought. Daylight would be here before they knew it.

All was quiet. Snaggletooth loved the feel of what had lately become a dark, dense, and very un-magical place. Because there were so few costumes remaining, the sense of gloom and doom had spread and settled over the entire village. It was harder to capture costumes now that they were on the alert, but since they were drained of energy and enthusiasm and didn't know when he would strike, he always ended up finding a few who weren't cautious, who were fool enough to wander the streets at night.

Tonight would be no different. Jabbering Jack had shown him where the girl and her costumes were. Now the witch was gone, making it the perfect time.

Snaggletooth slunk down Lemon Drop Lane to the edge of the forest. A light burned brightly up ahead. He pulled the MAGIX out, knowing all costumes and children couldn't resist candy. It was his greatest weapon.

He crept through the forest to where the girl and her costumes were sleeping around the fire. If he could get close enough to drop the candy with the other treats, it would be easy to grab a costume while the others were fast asleep.

They wouldn't know what hit them.

Kat was trying hard not to nod off, but it had been an exhausting day. She felt her eyelids getting heavier and heavier, but right as her head started to droop, she felt a tap on her shoulder. She jerked up and jumped back, landing in a karate stance, poised and ready to fight.

Jujitsu chuckled. "Nice stance. Where'd you learn that?"

"Ha-ha. Very funny. You can't creep up on someone like that. It startled the daylights out of me," Kat yawned. She just wanted to get in her sleeping bag and close her eyes.

Jujitsu Princess took the hot chocolate kettle off the fire and went over to the treats table, pouring herself a mug and topping it with mint-flavored marshmallows. She looked over the table, trying to decide what else she could have to keep her awake. She grabbed a piece of candy that didn't look familiar—but hey, it was candy, so she unwrapped it and popped it in her mouth.

As Kat was about to crawl into her bag for the night, she looked back and saw Jujitsu Princess standing in front of the table, frozen. Her eyes were wide and unblinking. She looked like she was made of stone.

"What are you doing? You'd better get comfortable, because it's going to be a long watch if you stay like that." Jujitsu didn't answer, didn't move. Kat ran to her, waving her hand in front of the Princess's face. "Hello? What's wrong with you?"

Kat reached out, and as she grabbed Jujitsu's robe, a huge hand reached out from the darkness of the forest and grabbed the Princess's other arm. Kat gasped, looked up, and saw dark eyes coming out of the shadows.

He stepped into the clearing, his top hat slightly askew, his bulbous pink nose and protruding fang much larger and more horrendous up close than Kat had ever imagined Dr. S to be. But she wasn't in Totsville anymore. This was Snaggletooth, towering over the two girls like a skyscraper blocking out the sun.

"Git out of ze way and maybe I'll decide not to hurt you. But zis one," Snaggletooth snarled, "is mine."

Kat was dumbfounded. She wanted to scream but couldn't. Her feet felt like stone and she couldn't move or speak. She thought of Dolce's whistle but knew she would never get to her backpack without Snaggletooth snatching Jujitsu from her grasp. All she knew was that she couldn't let go.

Snaggletooth took one step closer, then another. Kat looked around her, not knowing what to do. She was too scared to move. Her eyes landed on the table. Just as Snaggletooth reached toward Kat's neck, her free hand grabbed the kettle of hot chocolate and threw it at him with all her strength. The cast iron kettle hit him directly in the shoulder and the hot liquid flew out and all over his neck.

The blood-curdling bellow that came out of his mouth made Kat cower back, but it awoke Candy Cane Witch and the rest of the forest with a start. In an instant, other costumes started running towards the clearing, but Candy Cane Witch was already in motion, barreling toward Snaggletooth, broom in hand, ready to poke the long handle into his belly as hard as she could.

After his initial shock from the burning hot chocolate and blazing hot kettle, Snaggletooth lunged at Kat and grabbed her arm. But it was too late. He would soon be outnumbered and had to escape. Kat's whole body was now wrapped around Jujitsu Princess, and Snaggletooth was forced to let go or be caught. He knew the witch would be there any moment, and he wasn't ready to face her alone.

He looked at Kat with such spine-chilling anger that she had to look away.

"You will pay for zis, Kat McGee," he spat at her, and in a swirl of darkness, he disappeared into the forest.

As the other costumes reached Kat and her friends, Jujitsu blinked and pulled away from Kat, rubbing her head. "What happened? What's going on?"

Candy Cane was shaking with fear and excitement. "Y-Y-You wouldn't believe it! It was S-S-Snaggletooth. Kat saved you! She threw boiling hot chocolate in his face!"

Kat said, "I don't think it was that hot. It just startled him enough to let you go. But we got off easy. Next time we may not be so lucky. Let's find Dolce and tell her what happened."

A puff of purple smoke rose up from the fire, and Dolce stood in front of them. "I saw it all, Kat. DeLeche came to warn me. I tried to find Snaggletooth in the forest, but he got away too quickly. I'm so sorry I wasn't here to help. You were quick on your feet, Kat. Jujitsu is still here with us because of you. But you're right. Snaggletooth won't let something like that go. He'll come at you with everything he's got."

Kat shivered and grabbed the wrapper on the table. "At least we know how he's doing it. He's leaving this candy. It stuns the costumes just long enough for him to grab them."

"Of course . . . candy," Dolce said. "I'll spread the word through Treatsville to be extra cautious. But he may have something else up his sleeve as well."

Kat pulled her costumes closer. She realized she was far from ready to tackle Snaggletooth alone. The battle would be like David fighting Goliath, but they had an army of costumes to save, and they had to get ready to do it.

Dolce looked at them and said, "After that display, I think you're ready to move on to the next lesson. Try to get some sleep, and we'll start tomorrow."

CHAPTER 7:
Lesson 2: The Hay Maze: Prepare For Challenging Obstacles

WHICH WAY TO GO? OVER OR UNDER OR UP OR DOWN? DON'T GET STUCK OR TURNED AROUND OR IN THIS HAY MAZE YOU'LL FOREVER BE BOUND.

Anyone who has been in a hay maze knows it can be challenging, both physically and mentally. Huge bales of hay are stacked on top of one another and placed in intricate patterns to create a maze. Getting to the opposite end is a huge triumph because obstacles, challenges, and booby traps along the way slow down and confuse the unsuspecting player. One year Tommy Glaze got so disoriented and frustrated that he screamed for 45 minutes until someone came in and let him out.

But Kat McGee was not your average player. She was very proud of the fact that she currently held the record for completing the Totsville Harvest Festival Hay Maze faster and with fewer mistakes than any other competitor three years running.

She liked the challenge. Kat enjoyed thinking of creative ways to get around obstacles, like using a prickly scarecrow to get over the tar pit last year. Most of her classmates had to throw away all of their sneakers, which were covered in tar. Hay maze barriers and booby traps are often difficult, and sometimes messy or startling—like when Ellie Byrd stepped on the end of a rake two years ago. A fish head attached to the handle flew in her face. She hasn't been able to go near a hay maze since. Kat felt a huge sense of accomplishment every year that she emerged unscathed.

But the Totsville Hay Maze was small potatoes compared to the Pits of Gloom or the Swamp of Sorrow that Dolce had described. When Kat carefully opened and read the second lesson from the *Halloween Handbook*, she wasn't afraid to admit she felt a little outmatched. She knew Dolce was going to create a demanding and formidable hay maze, one that was strenuous enough for them to tackle what lay ahead on the journey to Snaggletooth's.

But although she had the help of her old costumes and the Spooky Story Hour last night—not to mention Jujitsu Princess's rescue—had given them some momentum, Kat still felt an impending sense of doom. She was no match for magic; she had no tricks up her sleeves. *What if the hot chocolate kettle was a fluke?* Kat thought with dread.

The next day, Dolce and DeLeche led Team Kat to the other side of the village. They passed the Leaning Tower of Pizza, walked past the Jungle Boogie—a jungle gym that was personally made by Jungle Jim from magical vines and limbs that swayed and wiggled—all the way to the Hobbit's Tree on the north end of the Friendly Forest. They approached a hollowed-out hay bale, the start of a long, black tunnel of hay with no end in sight.

Kat walked around the entrance, looking up and down and around, trying to see where the maze ended. On Old Man Patterson's farm in Totsville, it was easy to see the entrance *and* the exit, even if it was all the way at the other end of the field, which always made the unknown maze a little less intimidating.

"Umm, where does it end?" Kat asked, perplexed.

Dolce smiled mischievously. "This is a long and winding maze. You never know where you may end up. I trust you'll all be fine." With that she blew them a kiss and floated away.

"That's it? No advice? No words of wisdom? Not even a hint?" Candy Cane Witch shouted into the air, bewildered that they were completely on their own.

Jujitsu Princess took a few steps toward the darkness and mumbled, "I guess we're supposed to fend for ourselves."

Kat looked at DeLeche, perched on top of the hay bale, his huge lavender eyes staring right at them. His eyes closed; when they opened and the fog cleared, Kat saw a flashing deep purple light. *What's that supposed to mean?* She wondered.

"We'd better hustle. We want to finish this thing before dark," Kat said.

"Why does it matter? It's pitch black inside." Candy Cane Witch was not excited.

Kat reached inside her backpack and triumphantly announced, "Good thing I brought some glow-in-the-dark jewelry from my magic room!" She handed out the necklaces and bracelets, putting on a few on herself. "Let's get this glow on the road."

The costumes were too nervous to laugh at her joke.

They locked hands and started to slowly wind through the maze. One minute the tunnel was so high that they couldn't even reach the top; the next, they were crawling on their hands and knees and felt as though they were in a suffocating box. The soft glow of their jewelry helped, but it was still hard to see. The group made several wrong turns and ended up at dead ends. After a while, they felt like they were going in circles.

"I think we need to go this way," Candy Cane Witch said, pointing to a dark corner that Kat could have sworn they'd already tried.

Kat wasn't convinced. "I don't think so."

"I think she's right," Princess Jujitsu agreed.

"No, I think I'm right. We need to go that way," Kat said defiantly, pointing in the opposite direction.

Princess and Candy Cane looked at each other and shrugged. But as soon as they turned the corner to the left, they stumbled over a trip rope pulled tight right above the ground and landed in a pile of mud. They got up, covered in mud, and Jujitsu suddenly pushed them out of the way.

"Run! Hurry!" she screamed.

A hundred balloons filled with black paint dropped from a net above them. They ran in the other direction, barely getting out of the way before the balloons all splattered to the ground.

"The rope must have tripped a trap that released them," Jujitsu said.

Kat felt horrible. "I'm so sorry. You were right. We should have gone the other way." She was bossy and pushy, which led them straight into the trap.

"We all make mistakes, Kat," Candy Cane said softly, squeezing her hand. They hurried in the other direction. Sure enough, as soon as they turned the corner, they saw a smiling jack-o-lantern staring at them, grunting and leaning slightly as if to point toward a corridor into which they were obviously supposed to go.

As they walked, the corridor started to get smaller and smaller. First they had to hunch over, then they bent their knees almost to the ground. Finally they were on their hands and knees, crawling through a tunnel of hay instead of a large passageway. As they struggled through the tiny crawlspace, Kat started to get claustrophobic, like when her brother Abe had asked her to be his magician's assistant and locked her in a trunk in the attic for two whole hours. Thank goodness Gram had noticed she was missing for dinner or she might still be there. Kat needed to get out of here, and quickly.

They were practically flat to the ground now, inching along on their elbows at a snail's pace. Kat couldn't turn around so she yelled back at the others, "I think I see a space ahead!" She pushed and pulled more quickly. At the end she could finally stand.

The others quickly followed, crawling into in a large circular room where hay bales surrounded them. Three openings, like doorways into the hay, stood before them. The sun was already beginning to set and Kat noticed the brightness in her necklace starting to fade.

"We don't have time to waste, so we better pick the right one. Any ideas?"

"Door Number Three it is!" Kat and her posse headed through the passageway furthest to the right for no other reason than Princess Jujitsu winning *rock, paper, scissors,* so she got to pick. *Nothing like leaving it up to chance!* Kat thought.

They started down the path, which narrowed as they walked further. Soon it was so narrow they were in a single-file line. Their shoulders brushed the hay walls, like it was squeezing them ever more tightly together.

Kat looked back and tried to make a joke. "Snug as a bug in a . . . RUUUUUUUUUU . . . " Her voice trailed off in a scream as she fell into the darkness.

BOING! Candy Cane, next in line, slowed and felt in front of her for the drop. When she got to the edge, she looked down and saw Kat, fifteen feet below, as if she had just dived into a pool with no water and was resting at the bottom.

"I'm okay. I landed on some bubble thingamajig," Kat said, standing. The ground was a little slippery like a slide and bouncy like a trampoline. She tried to poke her finger through it; when she couldn't, the surface just popped back in place.

"Should I jump too? That sounded fun!" Candy Cane asked.

"No! Wait! Sheesh. Wait until we figure out how to get Kat out. Or where we're supposed to go next," Princess Jujitsu reasoned. She was always very practical.

"She's right," Kat yelled up." Can you see anything from up there?"

Candy Cane looked straight ahead, but it was dark and she couldn't make much out. Princess Jujitsu, stuck behind her in the narrow passage, tried to peer over her shoulder.

"Maybe I should get in front."

"What? You don't think I can figure it out?"

"I didn't say that," Jujitsu said.

"Then hold your horses," Candy Cane Witch said emphatically. She squinted her eyes, trying to see across the deep ravine, or hole, or whatever it was.

And then she spotted it.

"Look! Look! Over there! Straight across! A purple light!"

"Really?" Kat shouted. "That must be the end! That's what DeLeche was showing us. How do we get there?"

Candy Cane and Jujitsu waited for the light to return. It circled like a lighthouse lamp. When it came around again, it lit up the area surrounding them. Kat was in a humungous round crater in the ground, a hole, deep and wide enough to house a hot air balloon. Above it was a circle of trees . . . trees of Gummy Bears. The colorful bears hung like fruit from gummy branches.

"Gummy Bear Grove! I know exactly where we are! Wow. We covered a lot of ground," Jujitsu Princess said, surprised.

"But we can't get over there—" Candy Cane started.

"Without going down there," Jujitsu Princess finished her thought.

There was no way out of the narrow hay passage except down into the hole, but if they could somehow climb up the other side, they could easily reach the flashing light, which they hoped was the end.

Kat looked around her and smelled something sweet. *Of course!* She thought.

"That's it! That's what this bubble is: one big Gummy Bear!"

"Yum!" The costumes said in unison.

Kat looked up at them and then at the other side. She couldn't see the light or the trees. "Let me try to climb up on my own first. You guys stay put."

"Don't be ridiculous. Unless you can stretch your legs or arms 20 feet, you're not going anywhere. Here we come," Candy Cane said, looking around to see if there was anything they could use to get out of the pit.

Hay. Lots of hay. Candy Cane grabbed as much as she could stuff into her cape, turning it into a big pillow and tying it to her broom.

Candy Cane jumped out, holding her broom above her head and trying to use her hay-filled cape as a sort of parachute. "Geronimooooooo!!"

Jujitsu jumped without the same fanfare, but landed safely just the same. They ran over to Kat, who was still trying to climb up on her own. It was impossible. The walls of the crater were slick and cold, almost like an icicle that wasn't wet or melting. Kat couldn't find any footholds, and she kicked the wall in frustration. She was used to doing all things Halloween on her own, but this maze was quickly teaching her that she needed some help . . . big time.

Candy Cane popped up. "I got it. We need to make a human/costume ladder."

"This thing isn't flat or firm enough. We'll fall," Jujitsu reasoned.

"True," Kat said. "Unless we bounce with it."

"And we launch whoever is on top to the edge . . . " Candy Cane continued.

"And use your cape filled with hay to cushion the landing!" Kat finished.

Jujitsu looked skeptical, but they had no choice. "I guess I'm the anchor."

She got as close as she could to the slick wall and put her hands on it for support. Candy Cane climbed to stand on her shoulders and did the same, bracing her hands on the wall. Kat climbed up to the top, Candy Cane's hay-filled cape in her backpack, and stood on Candy Cane's shoulders. Candy Cane grabbed Kat's ankles so she could shoot her up and forward.

Kat could see the grass of Gummy Bear Grove above her, but it was still a few feet away. Jujitsu started to bend and straighten her knees, like a pogo stick, to move with the Gummy Bear bubble, gaining momentum.

"On three," she told them. "One. Two. THREE!"

As she yelled she jumped as high as she could; Candy Cane simultaneously jumped and threw Kat with all their combined momentum. As soon as she let go, Candy Cane fell backwards off of Jujitsu's shoulders into the bubble, landing with a soft bounce. They stood and looked up.

THUMP.

"Kat? Are you okay?"

No answer.

Kat landed hard but luckily had the hay-filled backpack to soften the fall. *Holy Cannoli*, she thought. *It actually worked!*

Ahead, she saw the purple lighthouse light turning. They were so close! Before she celebrated, though, she needed to figure out how to get Candy Cane and Jujitsu Princess out of the pit as well.

Frantically, she looked around to see what she could use. *Duh! I'm in a Gummy Grove.* She ran to the nearest Gummy Bear tree, tore off the longest gummy branches she could find, and tied them together.

Kat ran over to the edge of the massive hole and yelled down, "I made it! I'm okay. I'm going to lower these branches. They're from the Gummy trees, so they should stretch. Once you grab it, hold on tight."

She felt the gummy rope tighten and knew they had a hold of it. Slowly and carefully, Kat backed up towards the purple light, not wanting to tear the gummy branch or stretch it any further. One step at a time . . . this had to work.

Finally, she saw fingers come up over the edge. The load suddenly lifted, and without the weight of the costumes, Kat fell back to the ground. She stood and rushed back to the edge. Candy Cane was holding on as tightly as she could. Jujitsu hung from her ankles. Kat lay on the ground right next to the edge, and reached over her head and grabbed the nearest Gummy tree with both hands.

"Grab my feet and I'll pull you up," she yelled to Candy Cane Witch.

"Are you sure you can pull us both?"

"Just do it!"

Candy Cane reached for Kat's ankles, and Kat bent her knees, used every ounce of strength she could muster, and pulled herself closer to the tree, dragging the costumes up and out of the crater. Once firmly on the ground, Candy Cane

Witch crawled forward to help Jujitsu. They all collapsed on the ground, exhausted.

The purple light turned around again, and started to rotate more quickly. It spun faster and faster, so fast that sparks started to fly. More and more sparks flew, until the light exploded in the air like a firework, light and smoke bursting in front of them in shades of purple and lavender and violet and maroon.

When the smoke cleared, Dolce stood at their feet.

"You made it," she purred. "I'm very impressed."

"Wow. That was hard, even for me," Jujitsu Princess admitted.

Kat looked around, confused. "Yeah, it was brutal, but I don't get it. How was that supposed to prepare us for Snaggletooth's?"

Dolce smiled, patiently. "Ah sweets, don't you see? How did you find your way around? How did you get out of the Gummy Pit? Everything you overcame, you did with CREATIVITY and TEAMWORK. That's what you must take with you, the ability to trust and learn from each other.

"Now, don't lose focus. You have one more lesson, so we must get going."

The sun had set, twilight had faded, but there was no moon in the sky. It was dark and cold, and Kat was tired. They all were. But they had one final lesson. She looked at the costumes, and they nodded.

Kat peered around at Gummy Bear Grove, up at the sky, and at Dolce . . . and smiled. "Darkness descending on Treatsville. Didn't you say that's when all the fun begins?"

Snaggletooth stared at the costumes, his beady eyes boring into them as he paced across the floor, his fang protruding from his mouth. How could he have let a little hot chocolate get to him? Snaggletooth was angry with himself, and he took it out on the costumes. He put duct tape over Little Bo Peep's mouth just for yawning. Happy the Dwarf smiled at him, which—being Happy— the poor dwarf couldn't help but do, and Dr. S hit him over the head for it.

Glaring and mumbling, he went around and tightened the chains and ropes on every costume, so not only were they listless and weak, but he heard pain and discomfort in their whines. Casper the Fluorescently Friendly Ghost was on his last leg in the cage in the corner, and that made Snaggletooth feel better.

Soon the costumes would have no Halloween magic left in them at all. He was nearly finished with the final touches on the Halloween Hater potion. With the costumes on *his* side, he would be able to end Halloween not just in Treatsville, but everywhere.

But he was running out of time to stop the girl. He had to come up with something good—something final. And he had to do it fast.

He walked downstairs to his lab and looked at Jabbering Jack. "Git me ze Gatekeeper. Now." He twirled his thick eyebrows, an evil gleam in his eye.

"It would be my pleasure," Jabbering Jack replied.

Snaggletooth took off the pumpkin's top and peered inside once again.

CHAPTER 8:

Lesson 3: The Haunted House: Prepare For Startling Horrors

GHOSTS AND ZOMBIES, GHOULS AND MORE . . .
GET THROUGH THE HAUNTED HOUSE OR BE IN
TREATSVILLE NO MORE. IF YOU FEEL LIKE YOU'RE
SHRINKING YOU BETTER START THINKING WHAT
BOOK COULD BE A DOOR.

The Treatsville Haunted House was legendary. It was the kind of haunted house about which people wrote books and made movies and told stories to their grandchildren . . . and it was not for the faint of heart.

The final lesson in the *Halloween Handbook* would prepare Kat and the costumes for startling horrors, not by hearing or talking about them in stories, but by actually experiencing them firsthand: being face-to-face with darkness, terror, and pure fright and coming out unscarred and stronger for it.

Dolce knew that if Kat and the costumes could make it through the Haunted House without running out screaming for their lives they might just have a chance to make it up the Hill of Haunts and save Treatsville. The Haunted House was one of the few places Snaggletooth had not touched. Even he seemed to be scared of it.

The frazzled bunch headed across the village in silence, like warriors preparing for battle. A chill went through the air, and they looked at each other, an unspoken sadness passing between them: Another costume had disappeared.

Kat tried to focus. They had come so far. They had to finish their training. If they left for Snaggletooth's in the morning, they still had time to reach him before Halloween.

Before all the magic disappeared forever.

Kat's old costumes, like almost all the costumes in Treatsville, had been to several workshops at the Ghost and Goblin Haunted House School, and to several copycat haunted houses that had popped up around town. So they should have known exactly what to expect. They knew ghosts and goblins and vampires would be lurking around every corner to frighten them—after all, that was their job—but what they *didn't* know was what they dreaded most as they headed up the old, creaking steps to the front door.

"This is where I leave you," Dolce said, turning around to go. "Remember what you've learned. Remember that you have each other. And remember: Things are never as scary as they first seem."

With that, she blew a kiss into the air and disappeared. Kat pulled the costumes into a huddle. "We can do this," she whispered. "One last test, and then nothing can stop us."

She put her hand in the center for another Team Kat pile, except they all whispered as they threw their hands up, "Go Team Kat."

They walked toward the large, looming door, but as Kat reached out to the doorknob, the door opened on its own. A nefarious, taunting voice echoed from inside, "Come in, come in . . . if you dare."

The three girls moved as one closely clustered unit as they walked into the foyer. The door immediately slammed behind them, leaving the room pitch dark.

"Now what?" Candy Cane Witch asked in the darkened silence.

Another door creaked open; the light of a single match beckoned them inside. Kat could see a ghostly white hand holding the match, but couldn't make out an arm beyond the hand.

Going into the darkness didn't scare Kat as much as it did before the dark of the hay maze, but the bodiless hand asking her to follow it made her a tad more apprehensive in this particular instance.

"Stay together," she said, even though they were all still in a tightly knit huddle.

The second room seemed tiny compared to the first. The door closed again, this time creaking slowly shut. The match and the hand had disappeared, and it was silent. Kat started to hear heavy breathing.

"Is that you, Princess?" she asked hopefully.

"I think I stopped breathing the minute we walked in the door."

Kat reached out into the darkness, hoping to feel a wall or something to show her where to go next. Her hand brushed against cloth. A shirt, a body . . .

Was that a person?!?

Before she could scream, a blindingly white light flashed for a nanosecond. Kat and the costumes saw that they were completely surrounded by vampires, six of them, pressing their bodies up to them.

Kat and the costumes couldn't reach up because the ceiling was right above their heads. They couldn't bend down because they were too close together to move.

"AAAGGGGGGHHHHH!" they screamed.

One of the vampires uttered the age-old phrase no ten-year-old wants to hear, "I've come to suck your blood!"

A festering laugh followed, but still no movement. In fact, all they could hear was licking and slurping and swallowing, as if the vampires were licking their chops, just waiting to dig into their flesh.

Kat tried to settle herself. They could get out of this, but she had to stay calm enough to think. The room was so small that no one could move. *Or maybe,* she thought, *the vampires weren't **able** to move.* If they could, wouldn't one have grabbed them by now?

Plus, every haunted house Kat had ever been in had a way out. In the midst of chaos and screaming children, there was always a door, a passageway, something that led to the next room.

"Start feeling along the walls! Doorknobs, light switches, buttons, anything. Reach around the vampires or push into them. Just try to move and find a way out of here." Kat put a hand up to protect her face just in case a set of vampire teeth came near her, and then pushed and grabbed, feeling for something that would lead them anywhere but here.

Princess Jujitsu was the first to shout. "I found a button! Should I push it?"

"Please! And hurry," Candy Cane Witch begged. "If this vampire's bite doesn't kill me, his four-hundred-year-old breath will!"

Jujitsu pushed the button, and they started to move. It felt as if the room was rising, like an elevator. But the vampires didn't rise with them. As Kat had suspected, they weren't able to move at all. The vampires stood frozen in place and could only frighten with their voices, which were gnarly and startling because they were inches from the girls' faces. But in the end, Kat and the costumes had been scared of something that couldn't even move.

Kat realized they could learn from this.

"We jumped to conclusions and went a little wackadoo," she said. "We have to help each other stay calm."

With effort, Candy Cane Witch stopped her chattering teeth and admitted, "Easier said than done."

The small compartment stopped and a wall opened from the center, like an elevator door. They carefully stepped out, moving around the holes in the floor left where the vampires had stood, and entered an extremely cold room. The walls and floors were concrete and metal, and in the center was what looked like an operating table, illuminated by a single light bulb. The bulb hung from the ceiling, swinging in a small arc, like a metronome for a sad, slow song. Back and forth . . . back and forth . . . back and forth.

The air in the room smelled like ointment and disinfectant, which reminded Kat of the hospital room she was in for five hours when she broke her arm in second grade. A sheet covered something on the table, and Kat didn't want to know what was under it. Kat hated hospitals, hated doctors' offices; she even hated the pretend operating rooms in other haunted houses in Totsville. She usually just closed her eyes and got out as quickly as she could.

A door opened, and Kat and the costumes heard footsteps approaching the table. A large bespectacled man in a white lab coat, with crazy red spiked hair, as if he'd stuck his hand in an electrical socket, came into the light and up to the table. He had gloves on his hands, which held a large spoon and surgical scissors, and his face was so pale it looked as though it was covered in baby powder. In Kat's opinion, he looked more like a mad scientist than a doctor, and a spoon seemed a very unlikely tool to have in an operating room.

"I see I have visitors. Just in time for today's surgery. Please, step closer so you can watch. I would love for you to see my work," he said, daring them.

His bulging eyes, which almost popped out of his glasses, were enough to keep Kat at a safe distance. Jujitsu Princess was the first to take the bait. She was genuinely curious about what was under the sheet. Kat and Candy Cane stayed behind her, careful not to get too close. Kat covered her eyes but peeked through her fingers to make sure nothing bad happened.

"What are you going to do?" Jujitsu asked, her voice steady and assured.

"Ooooh? Curious? Please, step closer and you will see," he said, luring them with a single curling finger.

We're being led into a trap, Kat thought. She tried to hold Jujitsu Princess back, but the doctor, or mad scientist, or whatever he was, didn't seem to scare Jujitsu. She stepped right next to the table.

The mad man in the lab coat threw back the center portion of the blue sheet. All they could see was an elongated piece of skin with a large incision down the center of it. The top and bottom of the table were still covered in the blue sheet, and Kat couldn't tell if this small, uncovered portion was human or animal, if it had a head or a tail, if it was fake or real, if it was or alive or dead.

"First, I make the incision deeper," the mad scientist creepily said, cutting along the line with the scissors.

Jujitsu Princess leaned in, practically over the body. Candy Cane Witch gasped and covered her eyes. Blood and guts was not her strong suit. Kat stayed back at first, but then saw how strong and fearless Jujitsu was. Wanting to be brave like her costume friend, she took a small step forward.

What happened next was so fast and frantic that Kat wasn't sure what transpired.

The mad scientist put down his tools, leaned down, tore the cut open and started throwing things out of it, spraying the room. Something slimy hit Kat on the cheek, and she started running and screaming. Candy Cane Witch jumped three feet back as a pile of goo hit her in the face. She took off her cape and tried to cover herself with it. Jujitsu Princess drew her sword and tried swinging it at whatever flew in front of her, but still got splattered with something that stuck to her neck. Everyone was screaming and jumping, swatting their hands in front of their faces.

And all they could hear was the Mad Scientist's maniacal laugh, "AHHH HA HA HA HA HA HA . . . COME CLOSER, MY CATS . . . COME CLOSER . . . HA HA HA!"

Kat stopped swinging and screaming and tried to catch her breath. Her arms were still sticky and slimy and red—but as she looked closer, she smelled something familiar. The medicinal smell of the room was gone, replaced by a scent Kat recognized. She stepped back and looked around her.

"Everybody stop! STOP!" Despite her efforts to get the costumes to quiet down, the shrieking and screaming and laughing seemed to grow louder as the frenzy spread.

"IT'S SPAGHETTI!!!!" Kat yelled as loud as she could.

Jujitsu Princess was the first to stop yelling. She touched her face, looked at her fingers—and saw mushrooms and spaghetti sauce.

Candy Cane Witch was hysterical, but Kat finally calmed her down by repeating, "It's just spaghetti and meat sauce . . . " over and over.

Candy Cane finally smelled her arm and shouted, "Oregano!" Relief spread across her face.

When they had all caught their breath, they circled the operating table.

The mad scientist stopped laughing. "What are you talking about? What are you saying?" Once he saw they were no longer scared of him, *he* looked scared. He jerked around the room, searching for a way to escape. Backing away from Kat and the costumes, he said shakily, "Stay away! I am a doctor and a scientist! Stay away from me."

Kat and the costumes moved closer and closer, and he finally turned and ran as fast as he could through a metal door in the wall. Kat had no interest in following him, but appreciated his showing them how to get out of the haunted lab.

Following the mad scientist through the door, the group stepped out into a candlelit room. A fireplace stood against the wall and a dark burgundy velvet rug lay on the floor. There was no sign of the mad doctor. They were in a sort of library; books lined the walls from floor to ceiling.

The large metal door slammed behind them, and they let out a collective sigh.

"Whew," Kat fell to the floor in relief. "That was nutso-nutty! Here I thought blood and guts and intestines were flying around, and it was just spaghetti!"

Jujitsu Princess agreed. "And he seemed just as scared of us as we were of him, once we stopped running around the room and screaming ourselves into a tizzy!"

As she spoke a book flew off the wall. Then two. Then three. When there were 20 books on the floor beside them, everything stopped.

The first book Kat picked up had a horrible picture on the cover of a monster's melting face. She grabbed another, and it was equally as startling: a green witch, her face covered in warts and with only two teeth in her mouth. The green witch stuck her tongue right out of the cover when Kat passed it to Candy Cane.

"Ew!" Candy Cane yelled, dropping the book to the floor.

"What in the world could these be?" Jujitsu asked.

Kat opened the book with the evil-looking witch on the cover and read the title page aloud: "45 Spells to Get You Around the Swamp of Sorrow." Kat looked up and smiled.

"What? Seriously?"

Jujitsu grabbed the melting monster book. When she opened it, a song started playing, "Treatsville, Treatsville, lovely lovely Treatsville, with treats-a-plenty and laughs-a-many. Come on down to Treatsville."

"That's the old carnival song. I haven't heard it in years," Candy Cane said.

A wind swept through the room, and the fire went out. Kat and the costumes looked at each other. *Uh-oh. Not a good sign.*

Then, the walls started closing in on them.

Kat grabbed the books, as many and as quickly as she could, and shoved them in her backpack. These books were not what they seemed, and Kat knew they might need them. The *Halloween Handbook* started to shrink more to make room for the new books. And then Kat remembered: The *Halloween Handbook*! Of course! *If you feel like you're shrinking, you better start thinking, what book could be a door.*

"Start looking for a book about doors or tunnels or openings . . . pull them out or push them in or open them. Try anything! And quick!"

The girls each hurried to a different wall, but the space was getting smaller and smaller. Soon they were back-to back, each facing a different wall, throwing out books, pushing them in, opening and closing them.

Finally Kat found a book called *A Door in the Floor*. She opened it and saw a huge smile plastered on the front page.

And as she did, a doorway appeared in front of her . . . not in the floor at all.

Kat motioned for the costumes to follow. "Let's go!!"

They jumped, and the opening turned into a slippery slide, faster than anything Kat had ever been on . . . definitely faster than her SlipNSliderama at home, absolutely faster than her favorite roller coaster at TotWorld, and unbelievably faster than the waterslide Gram took her to when she visited last summer. This thing was FAST.

They slid down, going around and around, as faces and scenes from their training day whizzed by them like objects caught in a flying tornado: Spooky Story Hour and the costumes in the forest, Snaggletooth's fang in Kat's face, the Hay Maze and Gummy Bear Grove, the mad scientist and vampires flew by in flurry.

In a flash of light, they fell through a cotton ball-like door at the bottom of the slide and landed at the foot of the old creaking steps, the exact spot where they'd started.

They made it.

"I didn't doubt it for a second," Dolce said, giving Kat and the costumes a luminous smile.

"Well, it was scary, I'll give you that," Jujitsu said. "But you were right. Things aren't always what they seem. We learned you can't judge a book by its cover." She reached in Kat's backpack and grabbed the books that were totally different from their scary covers and titles. "Better take these with us. They may come in handy."

Kat had learned that and more. "Jujitsu was so strong and courageous in there. She helped me overcome my fear and realize that's one of the hardest things to do: Get past the fear in your head that may not exist in the real world."

"And I have to remember to try not to panic if a vampire is in my face," Candy Cane added. They chuckled.

Dolce smiled and said, "Yes, Jujitsu, you will learn that accepting people as they are will take you far. Kat, a wise man in your world once said the only thing to fear is fear itself. And Candy Cane, staying calm will help you in many parts of life, not just haunted houses. I am so proud of all of you."

Kat looked at her and asked, "Do you think we're ready?"

Dolce said, "Well, let's see. The *Halloween Handbook* will tell you."

Kat pulled the handbook out, and it enlarged before them. Kat didn't even need to touch it. It flipped open to the final page.

PLACE YOUR HAND HERE AND YOU WILL SOON SEE,
IF YOU'RE PREPARED TO KEEP TREATSVILLE A
SPLENDIFEROUS, SAFE PLACE TO BE.

Dolce nodded at them. Kat and the costumes stacked their hands on the book, just as they had done with each other throughout their journey. The handbook glowed a brilliant purple, exploded into a shimmering display of fireworks in front of them . . . and disappeared.

Dolce smiled at the worried look on Kat's face. "Don't worry. That means you don't need it anymore. It's back safe in my tepee in its glass home."

Kat and the costumes hugged and gave high-fives all around.

"This is it," Kat said. She looked at Dolce. "We're as ready as we're going to be. In the morning, let the true test begin!"

CHAPTER 9:
The True Test: Trick-Or-Treating To Snaggletooth

Kat never performed well under pressure. She bombed her vocabulary test in Mr. Livsey's English class: After he called her out for daydreaming while he distributed the tests, she got completely flustered and couldn't remember anything. In the biggest kickball game of the year, her team, the Totsville Trailblazers, were just one run away from winning the Golden Kickball—and she kicked the ball directly into Celeste Talley's hands. So uncool.

The one time she held it together was at the North Pole. When Santa needed her to save him from the booby trap in Scoogie's Red Sled 450-FX, she was able to bring him back safely. Kat hoped she could remember that courage, because she was going to need it now more than ever.

After a good night's rest, Kat and the costumes were excited and nervous but ready for their journey. A smiling Dolce floated with them to the edge of the Friendly Forest where she would take her leave. As they walked they discussed and went over what they had learned from Courage Camp and the *Halloween Handbook*.

They remembered Spooky Story Hour and were prepared for the unexpected. They went over what they faced in the Hay

Maze and knew they were prepared for challenging obstacles. And they backtracked through their journey in the Haunted House, which prepared them for startling horrors.

But were they ready to take on Snaggletooth?

Kat, Princess Jujitsu, and the Candy Cane Witch hugged Dolce and DeLeche at the edge of the Friendly Forest. Dolce leaned in, lowered her voice, and said seriously, "Beware. Be cautious. Be smart. Snaggletooth's got a lot of tricks up his sleeve. You won't always know who or what to believe out there."

This only made Kat more determined. "Time to shake a leg. We need to get these costumes back, PRONTO!"

Dolce put on her most reassuring smile, and looked at the three of them. "I know you can do it. Before the clock strikes midnight, the official beginning of Halloween, I know you will bring our costumes back to us. Bring the magic back to Treatsville."

Kat, Jujitsu Princess, and Candy Cane Witch looked at each other in hopeful anticipation, gave Dolce and DeLeche one more hug, and started on their journey to Snaggletooth's Lair.

"Keep vatch on ze Hill of Haunts. Do not let zem up zis hill."

He waved them off and smiled darkly. Snaggletooth had plenty of his minions out to thwart the girl and her costumes' progress. But if they made it past the Gatekeeper, the Swamp of Sorrows, and his traps, he would need more. He needed to know their weaknesses.

He looked around at all the poor excuses for costumes in front of him.

"YOU! YOU IN THE PINK AND GREEN SOCKS. COME HERE." Snaggletooth pointed his fat, wrinkled finger at Preppy Pirate, who was huddled in the corner of the dark room.

Preppy Pirate had no energy left. She shook her head slowly and whimpered, "I . . . I . . . I c-c-c-can't. I'm tied to the wall."

Snaggletooth nodded to the guards. They untied her and dragged her until she was standing, barely, in front of Snaggletooth, who was back in his chair, trying to calm himself. He worked better when calm. He looked her up and down and said, "So . . . they call you ze Preppy Pirate." He sneered at her. "You know zis Jujitsu Princess and Candy Cane Witch, don't you? Yes, yes you do. You are all thick as thieves. Vell, you vill tell me everything you know about zem. What they like, what they don't like, what they're *scared* of . . . "

Preppy Pirate looked to the corner of the room, her eyes fixed on Casper's small cage. He tried to lift his head to look toward her but couldn't say a word.

"He can't help you now. Do you want me to hang you upside down by zose braids of yours?" Snaggletooth snarled.

Preppy Pirate shook her head, too frightened to speak.

"No? I didn't zink so. Very well, let's start with zat Candy Cane Witch."

Kat and the costumes knew they were looking for the point where Witches Brew River split like a pitchfork. From there, they had to follow the widest, darkest, and fastest arm of the river right into the Forest of Fear.

They found the pitchfork easily and started up the path next to the raging water. The forest became so dense that even in the morning it was almost dark. They slogged through puddles thick with mud and grime and dirty black quicksand, almost getting stuck three times. They inched along the path as slowly as they dared so they would see or hear or feel booby traps. It felt like they were being watched. Kat turned her head carefully. Dozens of bright red eyes stared back at her.

"Keep your eyes straight ahead and maybe they'll leave us alone... Remember the book said the red-eyed flying foulawunks won't bother us unless they feel threatened," Kat said nervously.

Kat and the costumes heard howling and huddled closer together. Around the next bend, a moss-covered rusty gate barred the path. A black-robed costume came out from behind it, and his white hands emerged from his long sleeves and folded in front of him. His face hidden, a gravelly voice spoke from under his black hood. "I am the Gatekeeper. You can go no further. Turn back now."

Kat said, "We can't turn back. Why won't you let us through?"

"Do you know what kinds of terrors await you ahead?" the hooded costume queried.

The three girls shook their heads.

"I will tell you a story about the Forest of Fear. There once was a girl who entered and never came out. The red-eyed flying foulawunks surrounded her. Vines came up from the ground and wrapped themselves over her entire body, and her screams drifted into the forest, unanswered . . . "

Princess Jujitsu interrupted the Gatekeeper. "You know what? We've heard plenty of spooky stories, and that one isn't so great. Plus, it's a *story*, and we're not scared of stories anymore, are we girls?" she asked her friends, squeezing their hands.

The Gatekeeper screamed, "BUT THERE ARE DEADLY ANIMALS, FANGED WOLVES, AND VENOMOUS SNAKES AND SPIDERS. YOU WILL GET BITTEN AND STUNG AND NO ONE WILL HEAR YOUR SCREAMS."

They looked at each other—and remembered Spooky Story Hour.

Kat stood up tall and cleared her throat. "Princess J is right. Those are just words. We are not scared! We will face every spider and snake and vermin together. If you will kindly let us through, we'll be on our way," she declared confidently.

And it worked. The Gatekeeper was stunned silent. Finally he stammered, his voice not as menacing as before, "As you wish. But you can't say you weren't warned."

"You got it mister. Consider us warned," Candy Cane Witch said.

The Gatekeeper pointed his white, withered finger at the gate and it creaked open.

After passing through, Kat and her costumes weren't as scared by all the sounds they heard in the forest. The red-eyed creatures staring down from the trees didn't bother them, and they continued on cautiously but bravely.

They tried to pick up the pace and finally saw a light in the distance. The rest of the forest was dark as night, so the light was like a flashlight, leading the way. As they drew closer, they realized the light wasn't from the sky at all. The brightness radiated from a most unusual structure in front of them.

30 feet wide and just as tall, in the most dense and darkest part of their journey thus far, was a metallic wall of trumpets. It rose as high as the trees in the forest, maybe even higher. There was no way around it. Hundreds of trumpets, of varying sizes and different shades of the shiniest silver, gold, copper, and bronze, were intertwined and magically sealed together as they rose into the sky.

Kat was astonished. "Is that a wall of trumpets? In the Forest of Fear? Weird."

Princess Jujitsu ran up to it, excited. "Cool. It's like the Tree of Trumpets, in Trickytown. I go there all the time when I visit my cousin, Karate Kid."

"Wait, Jujitsu. What if it's a trap? We should proceed with caution . . . or something," Candy Cane Witch said, doubtful.

Princess Jujitsu said, "Do you see any other way around?" But when she saw Candy Cane Witch was genuinely scared,

she softened her tone and smiled. "Follow me. I've done this a hundred times."

She got a good foothold and started climbing. Every step she took let out a long, extended note, which sounded more like a sick duck than a trumpet. Kat was not far behind, but from the trumpets she stepped on came short, staccato notes, like beeping car alarms. With her broom strapped to her back, Candy Cane Witch followed more carefully, trying not to look down. Her steps played a slow, melodious waltz. Jujitsu led the way perfectly, and once they got into a rhythm, their different notes together played an odd, jazzy tune as they climbed.

At the top, they looked out into the forest and back towards Treatsville to the south. To the north were the Pits of Gloom, the Swamp of Sorrow, and, far in the distance, Snaggletooth's formidable house. Kat sighed. They had a long way to go. It was also quiet as a tomb, which deflated their moods like a leaking balloon.

Then it happened. The minute the trio started down the other side, every trumpet turned black. All the brightness and glow vanished; each one was dark as night and slick as oil. The moisture of the dark and damp forest had created a condensation that covered the wall, and every sound from the trumpets was gloomy and low and sullen.

Kat and the costumes could barely see anything in the dark of the forest. They were going down blindly, reaching out, without knowing what was below.

"This is so much harder, and much more dangerous. Be careful," Jujitsu warned, as she neared the ground.

Candy Cane slipped twice and almost lost her hat, but luckily regained her balance and caught it. Even without their magic, Candy Cane relied on her hat and broom to keep her safe.

Kat was making her way slowly down when she felt something tug at her foot. She looked down and the finger buttons from a trumpet were wrapping themselves around her shoelaces, tangling them up and forming a knot around the trumpet.

"Booneybomb! The finger buttons came alive and got my shoelaces!"

Jujitsu Princess turned around. "Hold on. I'll come back up and help."

"No, no . . . I can do it!" Kat said, straining to reach her laces. She wanted to get herself out of this mess, but as she reached down, she lost her balance and fell. She would have tumbled all the way to the ground, but her backpack caught onto the head of a trumpet. Her laces were still tangled on the buttons so she hung awkwardly sideways, unable to turn around and unhook her backpack or reach her shoelaces.

Jujitsu Princess slowly climbed back up to her, hoping the trumpets would stay still, making sure her sword was attached to her belt. "Here, grab my shoulders. Candy Cane, are you almost to the ground? Try to hurry. You can stand below us and use your cape as a net, just in case."

Candy Cane wished her broom worked so she could fly up and help, but she did as she was told. Once Princess Jujitsu saw Kat had a good hold of her shoulders and Candy Cane was in position, she drew her sword.

"Hiiii-yaw!!!" She shouted. Swishing her sword, she deftly cut the laces that were caught on the buttons. With her feet free, Kat caught hold of a catawampus trumpet sticking out of the wall. Still using Jujitsu's shoulders for balance, she turned and unhooked the strap of her backpack. With Jujitsu's strength and agility leading the way, they finally stepped onto solid ground on the other side of the trumpet wall. A loud trumpet groan echoed out from their final steps off the wall, and then it was silent again.

"Zonkers," Candy Cane Witch said, "I thought you were toast!" She turned to the Princess. "Talk about good under pressure!"

Kat gave Jujitsu a huge bear hug. "Yes, thank you. I couldn't have done it without you."

"Don't mention it. If we're going to get there in one piece, we're going to have to work together, remember?" Jujitsu said with a playful smile.

They looked around. The day was getting away from them.

"All righty then," Kat said. "Let's go. Those Pits of Gloom aren't going to come to us."

Marching onward, they came to a giant tree in the middle of two paths, one to the left and one to the right. The tree branches rippled and danced, like a windsock blowing in the wind.

As Kat and the costumes moved closer, they saw an old wooden sign shaped like an arrow nailed to the tree. Flashing writing, like a neon fast food sign, read "PITS OF GLOOM— 1km—ENTER AT YOUR OWN RISK." Kat would have preferred "FRENCH FRIES $1.99," like the sign down the street from her house in Totsville, but at least they were on the right track.

They followed the sign out of the forest and into a cave that echoed with every step they took. It sounded as if an entire army was following them. The remaining afternoon light disappeared in the darkness of the cave. They could barely see the huge round pits in the ground, but there was no mistaking their presence. The cave felt like an enormous hole with walls. Getting around the Pits of Gloom would not be easy. Stalactites hung from the ceiling like rock and mud-filled icicles. The walls and the ground were slippery and wet, and the amount of space between the wall and the deep, dark, threatening pits was miniscule. Kat and the costumes inched along the cavern, plastering themselves to the walls like glue.

"O O O H H H H H M M M M M M M M M . OOOOOOOHHHHHHMMMMM."

"What is that?" Candy Cane asked nervously. The moaning continued.

"O O O H H H H H M M M M M M M M M . OOOOOOOHHHHHHMMMMM."

"Let's just hope we don't fall into one of those pits and find out," Kat said.

They were halfway around the first pit when a sudden screeching forced them to stop. Swarms of lightning bugs and teeny fairies flew up from the pit. The fairy wings glowed when they flapped and at only five or six inches tall, they looked sweet, almost translucent. But the flying pixies weren't as friendly as they appeared. Their faces contorted in an ugly rage, and the screeching was almost too much to stand; Kat and the costumes covered their ears.

Kat finally understood the high-pitched noises. The fairies were screaming "GO BACK" and "GET OUT," and the noise was worse because of the echo in the pits.

Kat and the costumes tried to push around the swarms and continue along the slippery wall, but the fairies' heads became bigger and bigger until the giant phosphorescent nymph-heads were practically covering the trio like giant bubbles, yelling ever more loudly and fiercely to go back. The glowering heads were still attached to the tiny fairy bodies, like giant golf balls on tees, just asking to be toppled off. Kat tried to reach out and touch one to see if it would pop, but the pixie snapped at her hand, trying to bite her fingers off, so she quickly drew it back and concentrated on getting through them.

Kat thought the yelling was a trick, and tried not to be frightened, but there were hundreds of pixies everywhere. She and the costumes couldn't see where to go or how far they were from the other side of the pit. She didn't know what to do.

At that moment, Candy Cane Witch grabbed their hands and motioned for her and Jujitsu to follow her lead. She smashed up even more against the wall, and pulled Kat's hand, drawing her even closer. Jujitsu inched along until she was shoulder-to-shoulder with them. Candy Cane threw her cape over them and slipped down the wall, deliberately and slowly. In the dark, with only the lightning bugs and fairies giving pulses of light, and the din of their screams creating total bedlam, and the cape hiding their movement, the fairies didn't notice the trio creep through their swarms.

Kat and the costumes finally felt the firm ground widen and realized they had made it past the first pit. As soon as they all stepped around it, the nymph-heads popped and disappeared back into the Pit of Gloom.

"Wow, I thought fairies were supposed to be nice," Kat said. "And I don't know if I can hear out of my left ear," Kat said, exasperated.

"WE SHOULD KEEP GOING! WE'LL TALK LIKE THIS SO YOU CAN HEAR US. BUT THERE WILL BE AN ECHO," Candy Cane shouted, everything she said echoing twice.

Kat shook her head and couldn't help but smile. "I was kidding Candy Cane. It was super loud and hurt my ears, but I can hear fine." Candy Cane blushed.

The group slowly inched around one small pit and used a rickety plank to cross another in a single file line. Once on the other side they saw a glimmering light ahead. They were almost home free: one more pit to avoid. It also spread wall to wall, and although it wasn't as wide as some they had passed, it had no plank.

"If I had a running start, I could probably jump over it, but since there's nowhere to run in here, that option is out," Princess Jujitsu said.

"If I was tall like my sister Hannah I would extend my body across and make a human plank. You could walk over me," Kat suggested. "But unfortunately I'm a squirt."

Candy Cane scratched her head—and a light bulb went off. "Uh, duh. Let's use my broom! Since it doesn't fly right now, maybe it can be our way across."

"We can try it," Jujitsu replied. "But that means we'll be hanging and inching our way over, and we don't know what's below us in the pit."

"Well, that's better than trying to tip-toe across and falling," Kat said. "But is it long enough?"

Candy Cane pulled the broom off the strap on her back. "It extends," she explained, smiling, "for when I have passengers."

Sure enough, she twisted the broom in the middle and it became even longer, long enough to reach across the pit. Jujitsu went first, sitting on the edge of the pit while Kat and Candy Cane held the broom in place. She grabbed onto the handle like it was the monkey bars on a jungle gym. Carefully, she placed hand over hand to get to the other side. Though Jujitsu struggled to climb up out of the pit, she finally made it with a huff of effort.

"We're almost there. Hurry!" she exclaimed.

Princess stood on the other end of the broom to hold it in place as Kat started across. She was glad that her neighbors, the Tanksleys, had a jungle gym, and that she'd played on it nonstop in third grade. She quickly made it to the other side, and Jujitsu gave her a hand to help pull her out.

Candy Cane was more nervous, even though it was her idea. As she dropped down to hang from the broom she felt a strange movement below her.

"Something's tickling my feet!" She yelled.

Jujitsu and Kat knew Candy Cane had a tendency to panic, so they tried to calm her. "Just bend your knees and keep going. Remember the Haunted House. Things aren't as scary as they seem," Kat reminded her.

"O O O H H H H H M M M M M M M M M . OOOOOOOHHHHHHMMMMM." The sound was louder and closer than ever.

Candy Cane started talking to herself. "Don't panic. It's just like Jungle Boogie in Treatsville . . . Wait. It *is* just like Jungle Boogie." She started rocking her legs back and forth to get momentum and finally swung her feet up to the broom, too, so she hung from her hands and feet like a monkey. This gave her more stability, and Kat and Jujitsu grabbed her when she got to the other side, pulling her up to safety.

"Very creative, Candy Cane. Good thinking," Jujitsu Princess complimented.

"Thanks. Let's get out of here. It's Creepy McCreepykins," Candy Cane said, relieved to be on solid ground once again.

Unfortunately, the solid ground didn't last long. The Swamp of Sorrow was foggy, wet, and covered with either dark, muddy water or tar-like ooze. This was the yuckiest, smelliest, most disgusting swamp Kat had ever seen, much worse than the scummy pond with all the frogs behind the Little League field in Totsville.

The last light of the already overcast, dreary day disappeared, and the sky darkened. Kat and the costumes took each step with caution. Should they try to wade through, not knowing how deep it was or what creatures lurked beneath the surface? Should they try to go around it? Would the gurgling ooze swallow them whole?

Kat knelt down to feel the texture of the ground. As she touched the muddy, thick ooze, two yellow eyes rose up out of it, followed by the unmistakable V-shape and scales of a crocodile's head.

Kat yelped and tried to crawl backwards. She knew the crocodile could swallow her entire body in a blink. She stammered, "J-J-J-Jujitsu, can you or C-C-C-andy Cane reach my backpack and grab the book about the secrets to the swamp? And no sudden movements, but can you still try to do it quickly!?"

Candy Cane tiptoed toward Kat, carefully unzipped her backpack, and grabbed the books from the Haunted House. They couldn't remember which was which, so Candy Cane carefully handed one to Jujitsu and looked through one as well. Kat, meanwhile, inched back away from the crocodile.

But with every inch she moved back, the crocodile slinked closer to her.

Finally, Kat was next to the costumes again. They huddled together, standing still, reading through the books with the crocodile directly in front of them. Kat thought it was studying them, deciding whom to eat first.

"I think I found something," Jujitsu said, flipping through the *45 Spells* book. "Here, you do it," she said, shoving the book at Kat.

"No way. I put my foot down at reptiles," she refuted, handing the book to Candy Cane.

"Come on, guys. Remember, we aren't supposed to judge a book by its cover. Hello?!" Candy Cane reminded them, waving the book with the monster face in the air.

"Stop with the sudden movements! This isn't a book, it's a CROCODILE, dummy," Jujitsu countered.

Candy Cane was surprisingly calm. She looked at the page again, and her smile widened, causing her chubby, painted red cheeks to look like cherry tomatoes. "Oh, man. This is awesome!" She exclaimed.

"SHHHHHHHHHHH!!!" Kat and Princess Jujitsu hushed her.

The crocodile had emerged fully from the water but remained still. Candy Cane turned, knelt not a foot from his huge mouth of big, sharp teeth. His eyes blinked, and Candy Cane saw something in them that almost twinkled.

She looked down at the book and read, "Wonkablooming twist and burn. Teeth of fear will take a turn. Sweetness cohoodle blankratop!"

He blinked again. And again.

And then, the crocodile opened his huge jaws and croaked, "Cooookie."

Kat was befuddled. "Did he just say cookie?"

"Cooookie. Too sad. Need cookie," the crocodile grumbled again.

Candy Cane stood and turned to the others, smiling. "I just made it so we could understand him, but see? He wants a cookie. That's all."

"Super. But where do you plan on getting a cookie in the middle of a swamp?" Jujitsu sassed.

After the last few days, Kat knew a talking crocodile shouldn't surprise her, and yet it did. And then—it hit her: Gram's black cat cookies, in her backpack! She pulled the cookies out and laid them on the ground in front of the crocodile. He stepped forward to them and, in one swipe, gobbled them up.

"Mmm. Cookies. Cookies, good. Better now," he grunted as he swallowed.

"Excuse me, but do you know how we can get across to the Hill of Haunts?" Kat asked politely.

"Mmm. Cookie. I get cookie, you get ride," the Cookie Crocodile gurgled. "Climb on back."

Candy Cane stepped up in a heartbeat. Kat looked at Princess Jujitsu and shrugged. They followed Candy Cane, and just as smoothly as he'd crawled out of the swamp, Cookie Crocodile waded back in. Slowly but surely, he took them through the swamp and fog and mist to the other side. Kat and the costumes had to hold on to each other for balance and support, but she was definitely happy to be up on his back instead of down in the ooze.

The Cookie Crocodile eased his way out of the tar-like water onto dry ground. Kat and the costumes stepped off carefully. Jujitsu hugged Candy Cane as an apology for being harsh. Kat was so thankful Candy Cane had been braver than the two of them.

Kat turned to the crocodile and squatted down. She had to smile. Where in the world would she ever encounter a talking crocodile who liked cookies? "Thank you. Really. We would have sunk out there on our own."

Kat couldn't tell if the corners of his mouth turned up in a smile or if she imagined it, but the Cookie Crocodile grumbled. "Next time, more cookies."

With a splash, he disappeared back into the swamp.

"Well, that's not something you see every day," Kat said, standing.

"Neither is that," Candy Cane said. She had turned away from the Swamp of Sorrows and was pointing to their destination.

DUMBLEPIDGEON!

When he saw in Jabbering Jack that the girl and the costumes had actually made it out of the Swamp of Sorrow, Snaggletooth knew he was running out of time. He had known the Gatekeeper would be worthless, but they survived the Pits and the Swamp! If the costumes on the Hill and guarding the door couldn't stop that stupid kid and her costume friends, he would have to resort to more drastic measures.

He would do whatever he had to do to keep them out of his domain.

Now it was real. Kat, Candy Cane Witch, and Jujitsu Princess stood at the bottom the dismal, steep Hill of Haunts. The hazy night sky hid the moon. Scattered in front of them in the darkness were old tombstones, decaying tree stumps burnt by lightning, weeds that grew larger and thicker before their eyes, dead, smoking grass, and giant thorn bushes that sprayed thorns periodically from their branches. The butterscotch bushes had long ago melted, becoming sticky traps; Kat wrinkled her nose at the stench from the hot holes of goo.

A dozen ghosts floated back and forth, protecting their turf. They were translucent, but looked more like zombies than ghosts. No expressions, no sound . . . just floating apparitions in a repetitive monotony of movement.

At the top of the hill, barely visible through the thick fog, was Snaggletooth's house. It looked so close, yet what they had to pass to get there seemed impossibly gloomy and threatening.

"No turning back now," Kat said with a gulp.

Jujitsu examined the landscape, trying to formulate a quick plan. "The ghosts are floating past those tombstones every 20 seconds or so. Next time they pass, let's try to get to that broken wagon," she said, pointing ahead. "That will get us further up, and we can hide until we figure out how to get around them."

The group nodded and followed her lead. Kat slipped and fell twice, but quickly got up and hurried to the wagon, hands and knees covered in mud.

Kat's mind raced. What would the ghosts do to them if they were captured? Would they explode into monsters and slime them? Would they tackle and suffocate them? Would they drag them away to Snaggletooth? Or were they merely decoys trying to scare them off?

If that's the case, Kat thought, *it's working*.

But she was resolved to finish what they'd started. She whispered to Jujitsu and Candy Cane, "We have to go for it. Look at this fog. Maybe they won't see us?"

Jujitsu nodded. "You're right. It's now or never. And we won't know what they're going to do until they catch us," she said with a sly smile.

"I'm ready if you are. Let's confuse them," Candy Cane said with an equally mischievous smirk.

They put their hands together and whispered one more time, "Team Kat!"

Then they jumped out and started running toward Snaggletooth's House on the Hill. Each ran in a different direction, weaving her way up, through the mess of spewing thorns and gooey traps, trying to confuse the apparitions of gloom. But all too soon the ghosts caught on and started to chase them.

They passed rotting tree trunks and piles of bones scattered in desolate piles up the hill. Kat shuddered but kept running. As they got to the bridge that would take them to Snaggletooth's door, two costumes jumped out and stopped them. One was the Headless Horseman, and the other was the Riddler.

Kat and the costumes were startled to a stop but didn't scream. The ghosts floated up behind them. The girls were surrounded.

But together, they stood their ground and didn't show their fear. Kat and the costumes stared back at the Headless Horseman and the Riddler.

Finally, the Riddler spoke, "Riddle me this. Why do you not scream? Don't you know who we are?"

Kat stepped forward. "Oh yes. We know who you are. But we've learned a lot in the last few days, and I don't think you want to hurt us. Snaggletooth is making you *think* you do, but you don't."

The Riddler turned toward the Headless Horseman,

confused.

Jujitsu continued, "Maybe, since we're costumes . . . and you're costumes . . . you're really not so different from us."

Headless Horseman and Riddler hesitated, but they knew their orders. The Riddler lunged forward and grabbed Candy Cane Witch's hat off her head and the Headless Horseman grabbed her broom.

Candy Cane slumped to the ground, as if she'd fainted.

Kat knelt beside her and said, "Candy Cane, are you okay? Hello?" Her friend seemed to be in a deep sleep.

Jujitsu stepped up to face the two threatening costumes. "You think you win because you took her hat? Well, she's stronger than that. She used to think her power and magic came from that hat and broom, but things are different now. *We're* different now. "

Kat looked at Jujitsu and nodded, taking her cue. She turned back to Candy Cane, gently took her head in her hands, and said, "Your power, your magic, is inside you, Candy Cane. It isn't because of a hat and a broom. It's because of who you are. We made it here because of you, so stay with us. Don't let them win."

Candy Cane's fingers tapped the ground. Her eyes fluttered. She looked up at Kat and said, "That's right." Candy Cane jumped up and faced the two bullying costumes with renewed vigor. "We think you're just like us, and no one, not even Snaggletooth, can threaten you or convince you that you don't love Halloween. No one can steal *all* your magic." She looked back at Kat and Jujitsu with a rejuvenated smile.

The Riddler was so taken aback by her words that he stood

and stared at her, mouth agape. The Headless Horseman didn't know what to do.

The Riddler said, "But . . . but . . . that was supposed to ruin you. That was supposed to take all your magic away. Snaggletooth said it would!"

Candy Cane said, "Well, I thought so too. But I listened to my friend Jujitsu Princess, and I saw my friend Kat, and I knew that together, we would be okay. That I would be okay, broom or no broom, hat or no hat."

Jujitsu didn't skip a beat. "You see, Snaggletooth is wrong. And if you're like us, and Snaggletooth has stolen your Halloween magic, maybe you just need a friend . . . " She moved toward the Riddler, smiled at Kat, and continued, "Who can help you remember why you love Halloween."

Jujitsu put out her hand.

The Riddler again looked at the Horseman, who was perplexed, unsure what to do. The Riddler dropped his head and mumbled, "But Snaggletooth says we don't need any friends."

Kat said, "That's not true. Everybody needs friends. We'll be your friends."

As she was about to give the Riddler a hug there was a SCREEEECCCHHHH . . . and the rusty iron door creaked opened behind them. The ghosts fell back; the Riddler and the Horseman hid behind Kat and the costumes.

Kat saw a figure approaching and knew this was the moment for which they had trained. This was their chance to save Treatsville.

CHAPTER 10:
The Legend Of Snaggletooth

Kat now recognized the giant form coming towards them. Following him were three ghosts: one a small round blob, one a skeleton with a transparent sheet over it, and one who looked a lot like the Ghost of Christmas Past. Kat and the costumes stood still and, seconds later, found themselves face-to-face, once more, with Snaggletooth.

He snapped, "Well isn't zat sweet? Everyone needs friends."

Jujitsu and Candy Cane looked at Kat, not knowing what to do. This time she was ready. She eyed her backpack and nonchalantly whistled.

Jujitsu stood right behind Kat while Candy Cane moved to stand next to her, leaving Jujitsu somewhat hidden behind them. The Riddler, still hiding behind them all, put Candy Cane's hat back on her head, and the Horseman slipped her the broom. She smiled and mouthed the words *thank you.*

The evil man looked at Kat and snarled, "Do you zink zis is a game?"

Kat stalled, hoping Princess J would have time to get into her backpack. "No, I thought you'd give me a welcome reception, since we're old friends."

"Aren't you a clever girl?" he growled. "A clever girl who needs to learn some respect for her elders." He motioned to the ghosts. "Take her to ze dungeon. I have special plans for her." He turned back to Kat. "Any final requests?"

Kat stood her ground. "Yes, I have one question for you. Why?"

"Why what?"

"Why would you do this to Treatsville?"

"Because there is a better way. We don't need Halloween. We don't need ze costumes."

"But why? Why do you want to end Halloween forever? Why do you want to get rid of magic and costumes and fun and ghost stories and hay mazes and treats and—"

Snaggletooth couldn't bear to hear Kat list the wonderful things about the holiday. He interrupted her in a fury, "BECAUSE. I. HATE. HALLOWEEN!!!" Snaggletooth fumed, breathing heavily.

Behind her, Jujitsu finally got the whistle from Kat's backpack and threw it into her pocket. Snaggletooth stared at Kat and calmly smiled a horrifically evil smile. "You made me lose my temper." He turned to Riddler and Headless Horseman. "You were certainly very quick to betray me and change sides. Vill you believe anything anyone tells you? Zat must be a flaw in ze Hater potion I will fix."

He turned to the costume ghosts and ordered, "I have ze best idea. Why don't you tie our new visitors together with ze Stunning Rope—since zey all love each other so much—lock ze two worthless costumes with ze others, and go back to your posts. I don't want zat sickeningly sweet vitch finding her way here."

The round blob threw a glowing lasso around Kat and the costumes; the other two ghosts grabbed the Riddler and the Headless Horseman and dragged them into the grim house.

The rope didn't even touch them, but when Kat and the others tried to move, they found they couldn't pick their feet up off the ground. They could move their arms and hands, but their feet were stuck as though they'd been cemented together.

Snaggletooth surveyed his visitors. "Now zat I have your attention . . . Ahh ha ha ha ha!" He laughed a frightening, evil guffaw that sounded like a cow wheezing. "You're running out of time, little one. Tick tock, tick tock. Soon ze clock vill strike midnight. Ze costumes vill still be here and won't make it back to Treatsville in time to go into your world. Halloween vill be over FOREVER."

He moved toward the door. Kat and the costumes, still stuck in the lasso, moved together behind him, as if a magnetic force were pulling them along. Snaggletooth walked in through the giant iron door.

Kat couldn't take it anymore. Without thinking, she reached out and grabbed Snaggletooth by his thick black coat. He turned, towering over her, but she didn't feel small or scared anymore, the way she had in the forest. Up close, she saw Snaggletooth's neck was still red from the hot chocolate burn.

Taking a deep breath, Kat poked her two pointer fingers into his chest and looked directly into his eyes. "What do you have against Halloween anyway? Why do you hate it so much?"

She looked directly into his eyes, furrowing her brow. Then she saw something completely surprising in his eyes: sadness.

"Zat is none of your bidness," he said, turning to walk away.

Kat softened her voice and begged, "Wait. Please."

Snaggletooth stopped but didn't turn.

Kat tried not to cry and kept her voice steady. "I love Halloween. I love making costumes. I love carving pumpkins, and I love the Halloween carnival at school and the festival in Totsville. But do you know what I think is most magical about Halloween?"

Snaggletooth looked over his shoulder at Kat.

She continued, "Do you know how we got here tonight?"

He took one step toward her and the doorway. "Vell, obviously, you made it through ze Forest of Fear—"

"No," she said, interrupting him. "That's the path we followed, yes. But we got here because we were a team. We got here because we used our imaginations and we trusted each other. We didn't judge anyone we met; we accepted them, and each other, as we are, weaknesses and all. I used to think I didn't need anybody else at Halloween. But getting here, I realized that other people are what Halloween is all about! It's about being together and enjoying the magic together, not all alone. That's how we came here."

Snaggletooth shook his head. He didn't want to hear it. He didn't want to remember.

But still, he looked differently at this girl. What was she trying to do? Why did she care about what he thought?

Kat saw a flicker in his eye. She knew there was hope. "And do you know WHY we came here?"

Snaggletooth grumbled, "Why?"

Jujitsu Princess and Candy Cane Witch put their arms around Kat. She looked at both of them, and as one, the three pounded on the huge iron door with their fists,

KNOCK KNOCK KNOCK!

They put on their best Halloween smiles and yelled, "TRICK OR TREAT!"

Snaggletooth paused, his eyes fixed on Kat and the costumes. Their pure love of Halloween was all over their faces. As much as he tried to fight it, something started to melt inside of him, and his demeanor started to change. He thought back, way back . . . to a time he'd almost forgotten, a time when he loved Halloween. Was it possible? "You came here to trick or treat?"

Kat allowed a slight smile to cross her face. "Yes sir! This was the hardest house I've ever tried to get to BY FAR, so I figured it must be the best. And the best houses have the best treats, right? And the best treats mean the best people giving them, the people with the most Halloween magic of all."

Snaggletooth stepped toward Kat. "You thought zat about me? About my house?"

Kat and the costumes nodded.

"You thought my house vould be a good place to trick-or-treat? No one has been to my house to trick-or-treat in many, many years."

Kat was shocked. "Why?"

Snaggletooth shook his head. "I don't want to talk about it."

"But this is the best time to talk about it," Jujitsu said. "You don't have to be alone. We're here, and we want to be here with you . . . and the costumes."

Snaggletooth looked down at them. "You'd do zat for me? Why?"

A big, wide smile spread across Kat's face. "Because we believe in Halloween Magic. And we believe everyone has it. And where there's Halloween Magic, there's good—even if you've forgotten what it feels like."

Snaggletooth smiled for the first time in years. This time, his fang didn't scare Kat at all. She smiled back and said, "If you let us go, we can start that trick-or-treating. Whatchya got?"

Snaggletooth walked around Kat and the costumes three times, chanting something Kat couldn't understand. But after the third time around, the Stunning Rope vanished. Kat did ten jumping jacks, just to make sure. Then she looked at Snaggletooth and asked, "Will you tell me what happened to you?"

Snaggletooth, head bent and ashamed, began his story.

"Vhen I was a young man, I loved Halloween, just like all of you. I decorated everything zat didn't move, I always vore costumes, I loved treats . . . but as I grew older, I looked scarier and scarier to everyone. I thought I had to do something to make people like me, so I started making candy. I thought since everyone liked candy, everybody vould like me if I made it. And I was good at it. Amazing, even. I made zis house into a sparkling, shiny candy factory. I came up with a fantastically unique kind of candy every year, and all of Treatsville *loved* me for it. I had more costumes trick-or-treating up here, even though it was so far away and hard to get to, than anyone else, hands down. And costumes wouldn't just trick-or-treat on Halloween, zey trick-or-treated every day!

"Until one year, many years ago, I made a candy zat nobody liked."

Kat couldn't help herself and interrupted, "What was it?"

"It was called a Doodledrum. But something went wrong with ze recipe and it tasted like smelly, dirty socks."

"Ew," Kat said, wrinkling her nose and lips. "That sounds awful."

Snaggletooth shook his head, remembering. "Oh it was. Ze costumes started going other places for candy, and not as many costumes would trick-or-treat here, or come here at all. I couldn't stand it. I was very, very angry. I fired everyone who worked for me, closed down ze factory, boarded it up, and disappeared. For years I didn't go into town. I thought ze candy was ze only reason people liked me," he said sadly. "So now I was not only scary-looking, but I couldn't make candy. Vhat was I good for?"

"Over ze years I became bitter. I was angry at Treatsville because I thought zey had made me feel like a monster vith no talent. I stopped celebrating Halloween. And I wanted everyone else to stop celebrating it too."

"That sounds horrible. No wonder you hated Halloween," Kat said. "But . . . " she hesitated, wondering if she should continue. "But did you realize that they didn't make you feel like a monster? They didn't make you feel untalented? Maybe they were unkind, but you made yourself feel like that. Just like you thought it was all about making a candy so people would like you, I thought Halloween was all about a stupid costume contest so people would like *me*. But the magic of Halloween isn't in candy or costume contests. It's inside each of us."

Snaggletooth dropped his head and nodded. "Yes, I know zat now. But I didn't back zen. If I couldn't have it, I didn't want anyone else to have it, either. It became easier to hate Halloween zan to love it."

Kat said, "But you did love it. What did you love it about it?"

Snaggletooth shrugged. He felt guilty and was reluctant to say more.

"I know you can remember something. Anything," Kat encouraged.

Snaggletooth finally spoke, "Well, I loved making candy, obviously. My bat toffee boggles were to die for. But . . . I also loved decorating zis place. I loved it all."

Kat walked up to him and smiled. "Those sound pretty good to me. Why don't we get the other costumes, and we can help you make this house look like Halloween again!"

Snaggletooth turned to Kat. "You would do zat for me? After everything I've done to you and ze costumes and to Treatsville?"

Jujitsu Princess and Candy Cane Witch nodded. They, too, were wary. Could they trust this horrible man who had cast a spell over their village and held their friends captive for so long? Was he going to trick them?

Looking at their worried faces, Kat remembered the *Halloween Handbook* and all she had learned about trust, acceptance, and friendship. Then she said, "Yes, I would. We will. You don't have to hate anymore. We're going to help you remember what it's like to love Halloween." She paused, and added, "As long as you do one thing for us first."

Snaggletooth smiled. "Whatever you want."

"Well, I'd like to find some of my old costumes and get them back to Treatsville so we can have ourselves a Halloween. And we have to HURRY."

Kat couldn't believe the transformation in Snaggletooth. He was suddenly a flurry of activity, but not in the cold, heartless, menacing way he had been before. He ran to the nearest closet and pulled out bags and bags of Halloween decorations, including twinkling jack-o-lantern lights in orange and black and gold, and told Candy Cane to start hanging them throughout the house.

Kat wanted to see the costumes, but Snaggletooth assured her they were okay. He needed her help, he said. He sent Jujitsu Princess upstairs with the keys and told her to remove the chains and cuffs and take the ropes off the costumes. Then he took Kat down to the basement, where he had everything set up to make the MAGIX candy: all of his vials and potions and ingredients he had been mixing and cooking and bubbling. There he introduced her to Jabbering Jack.

"Master, do you know what you're doing? Isn't she the enemy?"

"I've been wrong, horribly and unforgivably wrong. I vant you to meet my new . . . my new . . . friend," Snaggletooth said hesitantly. Kat smiled and nodded.

For the first time ever, Jabbering Jack didn't know what to say.

Snaggletooth told him, "We need to work fast. Show me ze best way to get ze costumes back."

Jabbering Jack sighed, sounding almost relieved. "As you wish, sir."

Snaggletooth took the top off Jabbering Jack and looked inside. He saw all the costumes of Treatsville floating happily up, flying back to their home. He put the top back on and looked at Kat.

"I'm afraid I can't do zis alone. You have any vay to get in touch vith your vitch friend Dolce?"

"You bet I do," Kat said. "Give me two minutes."

Kat ran upstairs to a mixture of weak, groggy costumes, a splattering of questions, and nervous energy. It was easy to see which costumes had been there the longest; they could barely move. She couldn't believe someone could do this.

"What's going on?"

"Are we going home?"

"Where's the evil Snaggletooth?"

Jujitsu had tried to keep everyone calm and under control as she unlocked and untied them all, and as soon as she saw Kat ran over.

"These costumes are still weak, but they want to get out of here. We have to do something—and quick."

"Still have Dolce's whistle?" Jujitsu pulled it out of her pocket. "Give it a big hearty kiss," Kat said, smiling. "We're going to need her, right away! Have you seen Casper? And Preppy Pirate? And Bride of Frankenweenie? Are they okay?"

Princess pointed to the cage in the corner, and Kat ran over as quickly as she could. Casper lifted his head, weak but happy.

"Kat? Is that you?" He barely could smile, but she knew he was glad to see her.

"Oh Casper. Don't worry. I'm going get you out of here. I'll be back. Promise."

Kat looked through the pack of costumes to see if she could find Preppy Pirate or her other costumes. She finally spied her with Green Crayon and Bride of Frankenweenie huddled together in a corner. She pushed through the mob of costumes to hug them.

"I'm so relieved you are all right!" Kat said.

Preppy Pirate was in tears. "Kat, I'm so sorry. I told Snaggletooth about Candy Cane and her hat and broom. He made me do it!"

"Don't worry Pirate. We're here and we're fine. But I need to get back to help. Listen for instructions and help the other costumes who aren't as strong." Kat started to run back to the stairs just as Jujitsu Princess pressed Dolce's whistle to her lips.

Clouds of kisses fluttered out, spreading widely as the most magnificent breeze swept through the room. The scent of lavender and cotton candy and vanilla swirled around the costumes; the breeze became a miniature wind tunnel in the center of the room.

Before Kat could say *Holy Toledo Batman!* Dolce was standing next to them.

"You called?" Dolce smiled at her.

"We did," Kat yelled, motioning her to follow her down the stairs. Dolce floated down the stairs behind Kat and stopped in front of the huge man.

Kat decided to break the silence and said, "I believe you've met Dolce?"

Snaggletooth surprised Kat by kneeling down, taking Dolce's hand, and kissing it. "Forgive me," he groveled.

Dolce had seen all of the costumes upstairs, confused, curious, angry—but free.

"Smelvin, you are going to have to pay for what you did," she said harshly. Then, her tone softened. "But what a pleasure it is to have you back."

CHAPTER 11:

The Return To And The Return Of Treatsville

After their brief reunion, Snaggletooth explained to Dolce what Jabbering Jack had shown him, and asked her to help join their magic to try to get all the costumes home before midnight. They had half an hour and the clock was ticking. He didn't have the time to conjure a spell to move so many costumes at once. Likewise, Dolce's powers only went so far. She couldn't get all the costumes on her invisible floating carpet alone. They had to create something pretty spectacular, and they had to do it together.

Dolce and Snaggletooth added a gallon of Magic Milkweed, a handful of Wake-up Wolligaggers, a bucket-load of Halloween Happyhugger Juice, a dollop of Memory Munificence, a splash of Excitement Elixir, and some Flaming Fogglywops. They stirred and splashed and fanned and fired, trying to use their magic and power to create something miraculous: the Fancypants Flyer.

Dolce told Kat to enlist Candy Cane Witch and some of her witch friends as well. Now that the costumes were free, Candy Cane Witch, the Witches of Oz, and the Witches of Eastwick had some magic back in their brooms. The brooms wouldn't be fully functional until they returned to Treatsville and the magic had been completely restored, but they had enough to carry as many costumes as they could hold.

"Gather the other costumes and meet us on the bridge, now!" Dolce exclaimed. Her usual cool, calm demeanor had become a flurry of urgency.

She hurried upstairs to get Casper, since he had been in captivity the longest. Although not quite his Fluorescently Friendly self, he was clearly happy to be out of the cage. Kat, Jujitsu, and Candy Cane hurriedly helped him and the rest of the costumes outside to the bridge in front of Snaggletooth's door; Dolce and Snaggletooth met them there.

They had just fifteen minutes until the start of Halloween, so this was their one and only chance.

Dolce poured the magic candied powder into each of their hands, and they spread out around the costumes. Candy Cane and the other witches surrounded them carrying as many costumes as would fit on their brooms.

"Take the deepest breath you can," Dolce instructed the lot. "Hold it for two seconds, and think of your favorite thing about Treatsville. On three, we will blow the kiss of magic candied powder over everyone. Hopefully the Fancypants Flyer will take us home."

Kat looked at Dolce, Snaggletooth, and her costumes and said, "Ready when you are." She crossed her fingers of her other hand behind her back.

Together, they yelled, "ONE! TWO! THREE!"

Kat, Jujitsu, Candy Cane, Dolce and Snaggletooth blew the sparkling powder over the costumes and they all, slowly, gently, came off the ground . . . and started to float. It was as if they were on one giant, invisible magic carpet, flying toward Treatsville. The costumes huddled together, nervous and excited, and sparks flew off the invisible carpet like fireworks.

Kat looked down as they passed over the Hill of Haunts, the Swamp of Sorrow, the Pits of Gloom, and the Forest of Fear on their way back to Treatsville. She still couldn't believe that she and her costumes had made it through each of them, and was relieved to be far above, next to her friends and safe.

But they only had eight minutes left. Kat didn't think they would make it in time.

"We are almost there, Kat," Dolce said. Once more, she knew Kat's thoughts exactly. "One last thing and Treatsville will be saved, thanks to you. Keep your chin up, and BELIEVE! We may have Halloween after all."

Dolce was right. Kat saw the outskirts of Treatsville: Gummy Bear Grove, the Haunted House, and the mast from the *Pirates of the Caribbean* ship sat quiet in a blanket of fog. The group of costumes on their invisible carpet slowed and flew lower as they approached.

Hundreds of thousands of miniscule glittering and shining balls seemed to follow the Fancypants Flyer as it drew closer to Treatsville. Each one exploded and floated down to the world below, tiny glistening bits of enchantment and playfulness smelling of candy and popcorn, sounding like giggles and screams of delight. As the carpet carrying the costumes descended, and as the costumes got closer to their home, Kat felt the hope and magic returning already. She and the costumes started to hear and feel and see a symphony of sound and movement and smell and emotion.

MAGIC filled the air as the world below them began to come alive again.

The Fancypants Flyer set down in the middle of Kaleidoscope Field. Immediately upon landing, mayhem ensued. Costumes streamed out of houses. WHOOSH! An Angry Bird shot up right into the sky, then descended, crashing happily into barrels of apples ready for bobbing. All the costumes rushed—some moving more slowly and weakly than others—to reunite with their friends: Luke Skywalker ran to hug Chewbacca, and the Monster High Kids busted out of the Student Lounge, scattering all over. Little Red Riding Hood came running out of the Friendly Forest to find Goldilocks and the Three Bears, and American Girl Dolls Saige and Josefina ran to embrace their friends. The Tasmanian Devil couldn't control his excitement, slamming into anything that moved.

"Hooray! It's working! It's really working!" Kat yelled. "Treatsville is back!"

Snaggletooth looked relieved. Dolce reached across Kat and squeezed his shoulder. "You did a good thing, Smelvin. Don't ever forget that."

He smiled and humbly said, "WE did a good thing. It's only because you forgave me and gave me ze chance to show you I really was sorry. Thank you, Dolce." He started to sob.

Kat remembered her wrong turn in the Hay Maze and her many mistakes during her journey. Leaning over, she gave him a hug. "We all deserve second chances, Snaggletooth."

Dolce gracefully floated around the field, adjusting her beehive, making sure not a hair was out of place. She blew a kiss, and DeLeche appeared next to her. "I believe this calls for a celebration! DeLeche, let's make some arrangements and show Kat what Treatsville *really* looks like."

As she spoke, the Treatsville candied clock struck midnight.

Kat knew not even winning every costume contest until she was eighty could make her feel better than she did right now. She stood next to Jujitsu Princess and Candy Cane Witch on a stage made of Pixy Stix and Fun Dip Packs that Dolce had whipped up in a flash of kisses and balls of light. The *Halloween Handbook* floated safely in a glass beside Dolce, as Kat had first seen it. The Muppet Band was behind them onstage, playing a lively jig. Below, Kaleidoscope Field was a flurry of dancing, flying, jumping, and twirling costumes.

Dolce stood next to them, beaming with joy. She knelt down so she was face-to-face with Kat. Her midnight blue eyes mesmerized Kat, and her ruby red lips parted in a smile. "You should be so proud of yourself, Kat McGee. You did this," she said proudly, gesturing toward the field of merriment.

Kat blushed. "Well, I couldn't have done it without my costumes," she said.

Dolce nodded. "That's true. You had a one-of-a-kind team."

Kat smiled. "What about Snaggletooth? What will happen to him?"

"Oh, don't worry about Smelvin. He was the problem but also part of the solution. He wants to re-open the Candy Factory, and ensure that *everyone* is always *full* of Halloween magic," Dolce said with a wink. She stood, turned Kat toward the crowd, and said, "Now, let's have everyone meet you."

It was almost one in the morning, way past Kat's bedtime. But she wasn't sleepy. This was her favorite day: the beginning of Halloween. Dolce blew a kiss into the sea of costumes, and the boisterous crowd quieted. Dolce started to speak, her voice suddenly magnified as if she had a microphone. "Friends and family of Treatsville, welcome back!"

Everyone cheered.

"This has been a rough journey for all of us. We have suffered and been frightened and made sacrifices, but now Treatsville is back! We will be bigger and better than ever!" Dolce exclaimed.

Cheers and screams and applause from the crowd.

Dolce continued, "Before we go and begin our most sacred day of the year and some of you travel into the other world to do what you do best, I would like to introduce Kat McGee and her Halloween Dream Team, Jujitsu Princess and Candy Cane Witch!"

The costumes roared in applause. The Wizard of Oz witches flew over the field and sprayed a rainbow of confetti and sparkles from their brooms over the crowd.

Dolce looked into the crowd and back at the trio of girls. "You all showed an incredible amount of courage. You used teamwork, trust, and creativity to get you through the Forest of Fear, the Pits of Gloom, and the Swamp of Sorrow. Then, when others would have given up, you exhibited the acceptance and friendship you needed to finish the task. Bravo."

Snaggletooth and Casper smiled and waved to Kat from the front row. Kat waved back and turned to Dolce. "May I say one thing?" she asked.

"Of course!"

Kat walked to the *Halloween Handbook* and put one fingertip on the glass case. It dissolved, just as it had for Dolce that first night. Kat brought it to the center of the stage and opened it. It hovered midair in front of her.

"There is one thing we learned that isn't in the *Halloween Handbook*, and I think this final lesson needs to be added. If that's ok with you all?" Kat asked respectfully.

The costumes clapped in affirmation, and Dolce nodded. She blew a kiss and a purple pen popped up in front of her. Kat took it and spoke aloud as she wrote the last entry in golden ink:

Lesson Four: Prepare To Believe

EVERYONE HAS GOOD INSIDE; SOMETIMES IT'S JUST FORGOTTEN.
SO BE KIND TO THOSE WHO ARE UNKIND TO YOU,
AND THEY MAY CHOOSE GOOD OVER ROTTEN.

Dolce brought Candy Cane Witch and Princess Jujitsu over to Kat, and they hugged. The full moon was bright above them, and millions of stars gave them all the light they needed as Treatsville continued its celebration.

Now this, Kat thought, *feels like Halloween.*

Everything was practically perfect. Kat sat on the mushroom brownie armchairs with her old costumes watching everyone get back into the swing of things. It was late, so most of the Simpsons and the Seven Dwarfs had gone to bed. But the Lord of the Rings costumes were just getting started. The costumes had a lot to catch up on from all the time they'd been away: tricks to plan, treats to distribute, masks to fix. In a few short hours many would be traveling into the other world, and they had to be ready.

"Tell us more about the Pits of Gloom," Green Crayon begged.

Preppy Pirate piped up, too. "Yeah, and you had to get through the Haunted House? Outstanding!"

Candy Cane Witch and Jujitsu Princess wasted no time in telling, and elaborating on, their story of getting to Snaggletooth's. The other costumes leaned in, enthralled by the tale.

Kat saw Dolce approaching. She got up, stepped out of the circle, and walked towards her. For once, Dolce wasn't smiling.

"This can't be good," Kat said sadly.

"Bittersweet, I'm afraid," Dolce said. "I know you can't stay here forever, but I wanted to give you something to remember us by."

A single lavender tear dropped from her eye. She wiped it away and handed Kat a miniature *Halloween Handbook*. It fit in the palm of Kat's hand.

"Just in case you forget any of the lessons."

"Oh, I could never forget those. But thank you," Kat said.

Dolce gave Kat a kiss on both cheeks and whispered, "You are a Halloween treasure, Kat McGee. Treatsville will remember you always."

Kat sat on the giant mushroom brownie chair and all of her reunited costumes gathered around her. She smiled, thankful, at Candy Cane Witch and Jujitsu Princess.

Beside her, Bride of Frankenweenie took her hand. "Are you ready? It's almost time," she said.

"Time for what?" Kat asked.

Bride of Frankenweenie smiled and squeezed Kat's hand. Kat didn't want this feeling of contentment and happiness to end. She felt a warm glow and looked down at the *Halloween Handbook* in her lap. Kat smelled a familiar scent of vanilla and pumpkin and cinnamon. It reminded her of Gram. *Someone must be making some pumpkin pops or black cat cookies*, Kat thought.

She breathed in and felt relaxed and sleepy. Her eyes started to feel very heavy. As they closed, she thought of her time in Treatsville and wanted it to last forever. Halloween magic didn't get much better than this.

CHAPTER 12:
Halloween Returns To Totsville

Kat woke up and heard footsteps stomping all around her. She opened her eyes and looked around. Some costumes were scattered on her bed, and her backpack was beside her, half open, a few costumes shoved inside.

It must have been a dream, she thought. Then, a sinking feeling dropped in the pit of her stomach. *Oh NO! That means the ban is in place! No more Halloween!*

Kat grabbed her backpack and looked out the window. It was almost dark. She had to hurry or her parents and Gram wouldn't let her go to the Town Hall to confront the council members.

She ran into the hall, and her brother Abe flew past her. He was in his baseball uniform. *That's weird*, Kat thought. *It's not baseball season.* Her sister Emily walked by in a dressy pink Sunday school dress, a tiara, and a wand.

"What are you doing in that?" Kat asked skeptically.

Emily rolled her eyes at Kat and said, "What do you mean, dummy? It's Halloween. DUH! Mom said I had to dress up if I want to trick-or-treat, and this is the best I can do. I know it's not one of your grand creations, but give me a break."

She went downstairs, but Kat stood as still as a statue. Halloween!? In Totsville?! She ran downstairs and into the kitchen, just as Gram was pulling another batch of black cat cookies out of the oven. She looked at Kat and smiled.

"Kool Kat, you're not dressed yet? You better hurry up if you want to beat your trick-or-treat record. Your brothers and sisters are leaving in exactly—," she checked her watch, "— seven minutes."

Kat was so confused. "But what about the ordinance? What about Dr. S and the town council banning Halloween?"

Gram walked over to her, put her hands on Kat's cheeks and said, "Oh, sweet child. You don't remember what happened? Well, no time to explain now. You'd better hurry up and put on your costume. Get to it!"

Kat ran upstairs. Her Bride of Frankenweenie costume was set out neatly on her bed. She put her hands and legs through the papier-mâché hot dog, pinned her mustard-striped wig so that it stood straight up, and slid the huge fake diamond ring on her finger. Throwing on the white tulle skirt, she ran downstairs.

Her brothers and sisters were annoyed that she'd taken so long, as usual. But Gram was waiting by the door to explain the McGee Halloween rules, once again.

"Whoever gets to the most houses gets a special treat. You have 45 minutes and not a minute more. Extra bonus points for going to Dr. S's house on Hidden Meadow Hill. On your mark, get set, go!"

Everyone ran out the door, and Kat took off. Never in a million years would she normally have gone to Dr. S's house, but with Treatsville still fresh in her mind, she was determined to go there first. She rode her bike to the outskirts of town, climbed the huge hill, and took the gigantic brass knocker and slammed it against the door.

She turned away from the door and could see all the kids of Totsville in the distance trick-or-treating in her neighborhood. *What a happy place. Almost like Treatsville . . . if there is a Treatsville,* Kat thought, confused.

The big iron door slowly opened, and Dr. S stood scowling down at her. He looked exactly like Snaggletooth! But Dr. S didn't register that he had ever seen Kat before in his life. Her spirits dropped. Maybe it was all a dream.

"Yes?" He asked, clearly bothered by her presence.

Kat gulped, then managed to get out, "Umm . . . t-t-t-t-trick or treat?"

He stood silently. No response.

Then his scowl broke into a huge smile, his fang hanging over his lip. "It took you long enough to get here, Bride of Frankenweenie," he said, still smiling from ear to ear. He handed Kat a small bag and said, "Happy Halloween, young lady. You'd better hurry if you want to beat your brothers and sisters."

"Wait. How did you know I had brothers and sisters?"

Dr. S smiled.

Kat had so many questions. "What changed your mind about the ordinance? How did you get the council to bring Halloween back?"

Dr. S said, "Well, let's just say I had to learn a few lessons first. And once I did, I realized Halloween is a very special holiday."

Kat noticed a twinkle in his eye that looked familiar and couldn't shake the similarities. "Are you sure we haven't met before?"

"I feel like I know everyone who loves Halloween as much as I do, Kat McGee," he said. As he closed the door, Kat saw a sea of thousands of Halloween lights he had hung in the hall.

Wait! He knows my name! Kat thought, walking towards her bike. Then she looked down at her personalized glow-in-the-dark KAT MCGEE license plate. *Duh, everybody knows my name.*

She jumped back on her bike, which was hard to do in a hot dog costume and tulle skirt. Racing down the hill she almost missed the sign at the bottom that read "THE CANDY, CONFECTIONS AND TASTY TREATS OF DR. S: SHOP COMING SOON!"

Maybe it wasn't all a dream, Kat thought, heart pounding. *Maybe I really did go to Treatsville?* She wanted so much to believe it was real, but just like her North Pole adventure, she couldn't be sure. It certainly didn't feel like a dream. One of these days, she'd figure out if Dr. S was really Snaggletooth. But now, she had to focus.

Kat made it to 27 more houses before time was up, and she was huffing and puffing when she got back home. Her brothers and sisters returned, and they all divided up the candy equally, as was custom in the McGee house. Gram was there to supervise.

They got to the small brown bag at the bottom of Kat's candy pumpkin, and Gus grabbed it from her.

"What's in here?"

Kat shrugged. "I don't know. Dr. S gave it to me."

Her brothers' and sisters' jaws dropped to the floor.

"You went up to Dr. S's house?" Polly asked. "No way!"

Kat smiled. "Yeah, he was actually really nice."

Gus opened the bag and pulled out a whistle shaped like a pair of lips. Putting it to his lips and blowing in, no sound came out. "It doesn't work? Lame," he said, throwing it back in the bag.

Kat grabbed the bag, pulled out the whistle, and studied it. *It can't be*, she thought. She looked at Gram, beaming. Gram turned to the kids and said, "Okay. Kat gets the bonus points for going to the House on Hidden Meadow Hill. She wins! She'll get an extra—"

Kat interrupted her, "Actually, Gram, I don't really care about winning. I think we should share the prize. And next year, I'd love to trick-or-treat together, as a family."

Kat's brothers and sisters stared at her like she'd just swallowed a live bat. They couldn't believe what they were hearing.

"You'd give that up for us?" Emily questioned, eyeing Kat suspiciously.

"You'd want to hang out with us on Halloween? But that's the only time you're cool," Polly said, surprised.

Hannah added, "Would you give us some crazy fun costume ideas too?"

"Sure! Why can't we all be the McGee Queens and Kings of Halloween? There's certainly enough magic to go around," Kat said, glowing with pride.

Gus and Abe ran to Kat and gave her such a big hug that she fell backwards in her hotdog costume. The kids started laughing.

"Kat, I think that's a great idea. A good lesson for everyone. Okay then, you kids scoot into the kitchen. I have a surprise for ALL of you."

As the other McGee kids ran from the living room, Kat hung back, looking at her whistle, smiling. Gram knelt beside

Kat and said sweetly, "Dolce is a sweet little tart, isn't she?" She winked at Kat and followed the kids into the kitchen.

Kat blew the whistle and Dolce's face appeared in a small cloud in front of her. Dolce blew her a kiss and said, "Prepare to believe, Kat McGee. That's what you taught us in Treatsville."

Poof! The cloud and Dolce disappeared, but Kat smiled. She would always remember how she needed Jujitsu Princess's help in the Forest of Fear and didn't have to do it alone on the Wall of Trumpets. She thought of the Pits of Gloom and remembered that as a team, they'd used their imaginations to find creative ways to solve a problem. She'd always think of Candy Cane Witch talking to Cookie Crocodile in the Swamp of Sorrows and remember not to judge a book by its cover because you never know where you'll find a friend.

Most of all, she'd remember that there is magic everywhere and good in everyone. Sometimes it's just a little hard to find.

Acknowledgments

I'd like to thank Saira Rao and Carey Albertine for having an amazing vision, giving me the opportunity, and making the entire process collaborative and fun. Their encouragement and empathy as publishers and friends were incomparable. Thanks to Rebecca Munsterer for laying some magical groundwork. Thanks to Genevieve Gagne-Hawes for helping me realize my paragraphs can sometimes be entirely too long and astutely pinpointing exactly what I knew could be better. To Caroline Noel Cooper for her most generous contribution to a great cause. To Kat McGee's Facebook Friends who supported my social media-challenged ways, pushed the thumbs up, and made me feel like I wasn't making a complete fool of myself. To my parents and all of my Corpus, Birmingham, UVA, and LA families, both in blood and friendship, for supporting me on a bumpy, sometimes meandering road to find what I'm supposed to be when I grow up. To Kat, for making me love Halloween again. To my husband, who helps me remember every day that I don't always have bad luck.

Matthew 19:26.

Together Book Clubs: Questions for Discussion

1. What do you think is the most important lesson Kat and her costume friends learned in Treatsville?

2. When Kat and the gang is in the Forest of Fear listening to ghost stories, they realize that saying their fears out loud make them less scary. What are some things you are afraid of? Does talking about your fears make them less scary?

3. If you could make any of your past Halloween costumes come to life, which one would it be and why?

4. When Kat, Jujitsu Princess, and Candy Cane encounter the mad scientist in the Haunted House, they realize he is just as afraid of them as they are of him. What are some things you are afraid of that could also be afraid of you?

5. How do you think Gram knows Dolce? Do you think she is magical too?

6. If you could create a land made out of candy, what types of candy would you use?

7. Would you have forgiven Dr. Snaggletooth for the evil things he had done to Treatsville? Why or why not?

8. What do you think is the relationship between Dr. Snaggletooth and Dr. S?

9. Kat and her friends quickly learn the importance of staying calm in scary situations. Do you find staying calm difficult when you are scared? Why or why not?

10. What is your favorite part about Halloween?

Halloween Activities

1. Kat McGee is an expert at making creative Halloween costumes by simply using materials from around the house. Design your own inventive, homemade Halloween costume by using old materials from around your house!

2. Treatsville is a land made from all types of candy, from the Gummy Bear Grove (made of Gummy Bear Trees) to the Candy Corn Bridge. Draw the craziest imaginary land you can think of, or try to make a model of one out of candy!

3. Kat learns that ghost stories can be way scarier if they're told dramatically, and with sound effects. Write your own ghost story, and then tell it to someone in the spookiest way possible.

About Kristin Riddick

Kristin Riddick doesn't look good in hats, but she seems to wear a lot of them. Her voice has been heard on shows such as *One Tree Hill, The OC,* and *Everybody Hates Chris*, and on-camera she was briefly seen on Fox's *Breaking In*. Before *Kat*, she wrote a screenplay, a pilot, and a lot of memorable thank you notes… so she's told. She teaches Pilates and spinning to stay sane and takes a lot of chances riding her bike all over Los Angeles because she gets road rage when driving. A native of Corpus Christi, Texas, Kristin graduated from The University of Virginia and currently divides her time between LA and Austin with her husband.

Connect with Kristin:

www.kristinriddick.com
https://www.facebook.com/AKatMcgeeAdventure
Twitter: @katmcgeebooks

Other Books by
In This Together Media:

Mrs. Claus and The School of Christmas Spirit by Rebecca Munsterer
Soccer Sisters: Lily Out of Bounds by Andrea Montalbano
Soccer Sisters: Vee Caught Offside by Andrea Montalbano
Playing Nice by Rebekah Crane
Personal Statement by Jason Odell Williams

Connect with us!
www.inthistogethermedia.com
https://twitter.com/intogethermedia
https://www.facebook.com/InThisTogetherMedia

Made in the USA
Middletown, DE
25 October 2018